GLADHANDS

By Andrew J. Krause

Some content too disturbing for young readers.

*****

I'd like to thank the J's in my life, Jules, Jim, and
Joe, for making me who I am today, as well as my
family for always being there, and Craig for showing
me how hard an artist can work.

GLADHANDS

I want to start this out with a 'once upon a time.' It feels like a 'once upon a time' story, though it's not. 'Once upon a time' stories start that way to tell you that they never really happened, that you're not supposed to take them seriously. Well, that's not right for this story. Everything in the following pages is true. Now, I know what you're thinking. You've probably read the back flap and seen the words 'giants' and 'demons' and 'vampires' and decided that this book is a nice little piece of fiction.

It is and it isn't.

Let me just say that if you can't see how a lie can tell the truth, then this book isn't for you. If you can, then let me tell you a story...

PRELUDE

Just like every other night, James' father, Patrick, read him a story before going to bed. It had been their tradition for as long as little James could remember; his father would read a fairy tale to put the boy to sleep. Fairy tales were Patrick's job; he wrote them and sold them to magazines, but only after they got his son's seal of approval. The boy had heard some of those stories thousands of times, and he knew them inside and out.

Lately something had been changing in their nightly ritual. Now, you may not be aware of this, but children are actually remarkably observant, especially when it comes to their parents. James noticed the first night that Patrick wasn't holding himself steady, just as he noticed that there was a sharp and sour smell on his father's breath. He could see what was causing it, the short glass that held an amber liquid, and he could see the bottle on the top shelf in the kitchen that it came from. Scotch. He could read that word well enough. Scotch.

What he couldn't see were the reasons why night after night his dad kept drinking it. More and more James would have to help his father get the story right; Patrick began changing things, and the stories became dark. Characters died where they should have lived, and lost where they should have won. Happily ever afters became scarce.

He tried what any kid would do; he got rid of the poison, pouring it down the kitchen sink. Even so, night after night there was always a fresh bottle there.

This is all a prelude, though. The real story began when James saw a ghost standing at the foot of his bed.

CHAPTER ONE

She was tall and pale, her eyes sunken and cracked around the edges. There was no mouth on the bottom half of her face, just a stretched flap of skin that wobbled when she moved. It was enough to send a chill straight down the back of James' spine. Her fingers were long and spindly as they crawled along the base of his bed. She was translucent; James could see his dresser straight through her, but that in no way made her any less intimidating.

Now, if it were most people in that position, they would have high-tailed it and run screaming out of that bedroom the instant they saw her. Our little James, however, was cut from stronger steel. He simply pulled up his sheet to his chin and tried talking to her.

"What do you want?" he asked, his voice coming out in a whisper.

She hovered over the bottom of his bed, her outline wispy and billowing, like hair in the wind. Her spider-leg fingers paused, turned over, and gave him a beckoning motion.

The room outside his blanket was abnormally cold, but he gathered all the courage he had and stepped out of bed anyway.

As any child will tell you, houses in the night take on a different personality. Doorways become great gaping mouths, and shadows form into claws tickling the back of your neck. Still, despite the ominous terror of the night, James walked after the ghost. Hobbes, his orange and white cat, followed at his ankles. The apparition looked back often, checking to make sure the child was following.

She led him through the hallway and down the stairs, floating a few inches above the ground. They passed through the kitchen, where the tile floor was cold on his bare feet, and then through the living room. James had walked the entire way unquestioningly, but he stopped as soon as he saw where she was taking him.

The door to his father's home office was ajar. In his childish mind the place held a certain sacredness; it was consecrated ground. He had only been in there a few times, and always while Patrick was with him. To set foot in there alone would be like stepping across a grave, the possibilities too horrifying for words.

Still, that was where the ghost was, holding the door open for him, staring back at him with those cold, black pupils. It was clear she meant for him to enter, to follow.

Again, you might be questioning why a little kid would follow a ghost. You tell yourself that if you were in that position, you would flip on all the lights and call a priest to have him exorcise the place. Well, this wasn't a movie, this was real life, and the kid's curiosity got the better of him. He swallowed down any fear he might have had and followed her.

The office was as he remembered, but like I said, everything's different in the dark. The empty leather chair behind the desk looked sharper, darker, even deathly. Around the walls shelves sat with books haphazardly thrown on them, stacked up sideways, many of them bent and worn. Patrick, long before this story ever took place, used to say that you could tell a lot about a person by their books. Never trust a man who doesn't have at least a few dog-eared and cracked paperbacks on a shelf. But I digress.

The centerpiece to the entire room was a large oak desk. This thing was huge to James' little eyes, a mountain of a thing, immovable. It was impossible for him to conceive that this desk could exist anywhere but right where it was. The house must have been built around this gorgeous solid wood thing.

That night, when he followed the ghost into the study, there was a mist coming out from the top of the desk. James couldn't see the top; he was always a little on the shorter side, but he could see this floating, roiling mist just being pumped out the top of the desk and falling down over the sides. And that wasn't the only strange thing about his father's office that night.

Though the room was smack dab in the middle of the house, James could hear the sound of chirping crickets and croaking bullfrogs coming from somewhere. It wouldn't have been strange to hear that if he were standing outside or down by the creek; but there? The walls were far too thick for it.

The ghost floated up above the desk and waved again for James to follow, and then the most curious thing happened. As though it were a trick of physics, the ghost turned, shrank, and seemed to be sucked into the desk, leaving a faint glow behind.

He had to use his father's leather chair to properly see the top of the desk, and when he did the shock almost knocked him off it. There was a bottle and a glass, both empty, that sour smell coming from them, but that wasn't what had surprised him. A stack of papers was scattered across the desk. One page in particular caught his eye. It was clear, like a window, with the mist pushing out the top of it. The sound of crickets and bullfrogs was louder near the page. Crawling up on hands and knees on top of the desk, James tried to waft away the mist, wanting to see under it, but it was too thick. Leaning forward, he reached a hand out to touch it, inching closer only as fast as he dared. There seemed to be an outline forming, a slight shadow, but no matter how he squinted or leaned forward it didn't come into view. Finally he worked up the courage to touch it directly, willing his hand closer and closer until it passed *through* the boundary and into the mist, as though the desk on the other side of the page didn't even exist.

With a sudden motion, the shadow reached forward and a hand grasped his own, the fingers that gripped at him spindly and thin. James felt lifted and pulled, the outline of his body distorting as his father's office fell away and the story swallowed him up.

*****

You might be thinking that I've gone off the deep end, that there's no way this could all be true, but I swear on my Aunt Sally that it is. Some pages have power, they can suck you right into the story; they're a thing to be respected. Approach every book with caution; you never know when it might change something deep inside you. But I'll get back to my tale.

*****

He landed on soft ground, his knees and hands sinking into the cold and squishy surface. The mist hung all around. Tree branches loomed overhead, looking very much like skeletal hands reaching for him. The sound of crickets and frogs chirped in the distance. Though he had never been to one in his life, the word 'bog' fit that place well.

A sudden and high-pitched cackle cut through the fog. It sent a shiver down his spine in a way that nails on a chalkboard would, causing him to crouch on his haunches involuntarily. James could see a faint orange light flickering dimly in the distance.

Above him a hole in the fabric of that universe held open, a small paper-sized portal. Through it he could see the ceiling of his father's office. If he were to jump, he could probably reach the hole. Turning away, he followed the path.

The ground made a sickly wet squelching sound with every step. It was a noxious thing, like making your way through a sewer. As the light got closer the sound of crickets and frogs stopped, an eerie silence settling over the path. A light shiver ran up the length of James' spine, but he was a hardy boy, and once he set his mind to something he saw it through. He continued on.

The light came from a small cottage. It would be strange enough to see a home out in so foreboding a place, but to see one like that was even stranger. It grew out of the ground and was covered in ivy, as though the land sought to reclaim it, to bring it down back into the depths. It was made of stone, the windows glowing orange from a fire inside. The smell of smoke was thick in the air, along with something sweet and inviting. There were a few gardening implements, old metal things, left by the side of the cottage under the window. This was not a place for neighbors and back yard barbecues, this was a place someone went to be alone.

James stepped forward to the window, having to stand on his tiptoes on top of a bucket just to see in, his childish fingers gripping the windowsill. Inside the cottage a fire was burning low under a black cast-iron stove. A table set for two was in the middle of the room, with two people sitting opposite each other. On one side was the woman he had seen in his room, but she was no ghost. She was flesh and blood, tied to the chair with a bit of white cloth wrapped tightly over her mouth. Her hair was jet black and fell all around her shoulders. She wore a white nightgown that looked old, so old to James' young eyes, but her face and body were beautiful. Her skin had a lively color to it, a pink flush on her chest above where the ropes held her to the chair. It took a minute for James to tear his eyes from her to look to the other person in the room.

The woman across the table from her was as ugly as the first was beautiful. She was an old woman, her skin wrinkled and riddled with warts. Her cheeks were filled with those overly large moles that grow black hairs out of them. The nose on her face was straight and large, with cavernous nostrils sucking in deep breaths. Her eyelids were hooded, half covering her small and beady black eyes. She wore no shirt, exposing her barren and empty breasts. Her stomach flopped over on itself, the wrinkles compounding, her skin yellow in places, translucent in others, with purple veins spider-webbing under everything. What hair she had was gray and greasy, sticking to her scalp.

The old crone was saying something James couldn't quite hear. He watched with a horrified fascination as she reached across to touch the young woman's face, her eyes barely containing a terrifying excitement.

Every instinct in James' young body was to flee the scene, but he couldn't take his eyes from the old woman. She lifted the beautiful woman's hand to her mouth, baring her crumbling gravestone teeth and tonguing one of her fingers. The younger woman's eyes widened with horror and she struggled against her bonds, but she could do nothing to stop the crone from tasting her fingers. The old woman sucked at them greedily, saliva dripping from the corners of her mouth.

James winced as the crone bit down hard, a trickle of blood spurting down onto the table. Though the beautiful black-haired woman was tied, James could see her face distorting with the pain. To his horror, as the crone leaned back and chewed with relish, the tiny bloody stump was all too visible.

A cold dash of fear splashed against James' insides as he

watched the scene, knowing that if he didn't do something, and quickly, he was going to have to watch that nine more times. As he struggled to think of what to do, simple gravity stepped in to help him. He shifted too much in one direction on the bucket and tried to overcompensate, causing it to sway precariously under him. As outsiders, we know that James' fall was finalized the moment that bucket tipped, but James' reflexes still tried to save the situation. Unfortunately, their only response was to shoot out his arms awkwardly to grab onto anything he could, tipping over himself and the bucket, as well as a rake, shovel, and hoe, making a lot more noise than he would have if he had just fallen.

Now, this should be a good indicator as to how stupid our reflexes can be. Instead of running and hiding, like a sane person would have done in that position, James' instincts kicked in and told him to freeze right there on the ground.

Of course the door opened and someone stepped out and saw him lying there. However, this was neither the crone nor the beautiful black-haired woman. This was a young woman with full lips and long red hair that trailed tantalizingly down into the crevice of her breasts. "Can I help you, young man?" she asked in a voice that trilled melodiously.

Her pale skin showed out from under the thin dress she was wearing, and James found himself confused and flushed looking at her. He had felt these feelings before, the catch of his breath coming faster, warmth spreading to his cheeks, his hands tingling, but it had never been this strong, this immediate. The girls in his grade had barely begun to blossom, their bodies still much the same as his. He could not help himself from running his eyes over her form, her soft and full face, her beautifully proportioned hands, the heave and gentle slope of her profile. It was enough to make him wobbly in the knees.

Luckily puberty had not yet fully hit young James, or his faculties of reason would have completely left him. As it was, he stepped back up on the bucket and looked inside again. The table was there, the stove was there, but the crone and the young dark-haired woman were gone. Even the plates and silverware were gone, leaving the table bare and clean. His eyebrows furrowed in concern.

"I said," the woman repeated herself, "can I help you, young man? It isn't very polite to go around staring into other people's windows." The lyrical quality of her voice excited him, and he had the sudden and desperate desire to hear her again and again. The letters fluttered through the air as she sounded them, her tongue dancing in her mouth. James tried hard not to stare.

"I'm sorry, ma'am," he said, stepping toward her. The smell that surrounded her was intoxicating; it smelled of cinnamon and vanilla, of freshly baked cookies and other sweets. His mouth began to salivate. "I'm not sure what I'm doing here. Where is this place?"

She smiled at him kindly, her teeth white and straight, her eyes open and honest, if a little curious. "You don't know where you are? You're in the woods, down the path. Why don't you come inside? We'll get you some food and something warm to drink."

He looked back through the window again. "Where did the other women go?"

"What other women? I'm all alone, so alone. My dear, come inside, we'll get you something to drink to clear your head." The entire time she spoke the smile never left her face. It was eerie, that constant, charming smile she gave him. He followed her inside, not really thinking, not really capable of thought while looking at her.

The cottage was warm and the smell of cinnamon and vanilla was even stronger. His head swam pleasantly as he sat at the table and she busied herself in the kitchen, putting together a plate of cookies and sweets that she set in front of him before pouring him a glass of milk. She did not sit in the chair across from him, rather standing by his side, always with that smile of hers.

"No thank you," he said, "I'm really not hungry."

She pouted at him as she leaned up against her cabinets, pointing her chin down towards her bosom and running her fingers through her hair. The corners of her arms pressed in, and if possible her breasts heaved toward him more. His resolve began to thin. After all, it would be impolite to refuse her, wouldn't it?

"No?" she said, "I've never met a child who didn't like sweets."

That seemed to resolve something in James. He sat straight in his chair, pulling his shoulders back and jutting his chin out. "I'm not a child; I'm a man. Dad said so himself."

"Well," she said, running a finger along her neck, "I apologize, clearly I've misjudged you. Let me get my *man* something proper to drink." She took the milk away from James and poured it down the sink. Reaching in to the cabinet she brought out a bottle that looked an awful lot like the one his dad kept on his desk. She poured him a large glass of it and set it before him. "Do you know what this is? Of course you do, what could I be thinking? You're a man. And scotch is what men drink."

He took the glass in a hand that shook more than he was willing to admit to himself. It smelled like his father. The woman's eyes were a vibrant green that followed his every movement as he brought the glass to his lips. If his dad could drink it, so could he. He took a sip.

The liquid exploded down his throat, burning his virgin tongue. Tears sprang to his eyes and his head swam, blood rushing through his ears, bringing the sound of the ocean. He fought the urge to cough, gripping at his knee. Why on earth would his dad drink that stuff?

"It's good scotch, isn't it?" she said, coming up to stand behind him. She ran her hands over his neck and chest in a way no one ever had before, her touch warm and soft. He swallowed hard, conscious of nothing except for her light touch and the feel of her breasts pushing against the back of his head.

Stepping in front of him, she began to toy with the little bow on the front of her dress, the white silk lace that wove everything together. James swallowed hard, his throat numbed from the scotch. He was tingling all over. "I'm glad that you came, it can get quite lonely out here in the woods," she said, pulling at one end of the silk bow. The knot fell apart in her hands, the two sides to the dress pushed open by her heaving breasts. They were suddenly free, hanging beautifully. James had seen breasts before; Mitchell had printed out pictures and brought them to Ms. O'Malley's classroom. But this was different. He couldn't take his eyes from the soft curve of them, the valley where they stood apart, the gentle peak at the end. She rubbed her fingers over them, rolling at them until her nipples stood taught. "Would you like to suck on them?" she asked.

James swallowed hard, gripping the glass tight in his hands. He was very conscious of how small he was; his fingers couldn't quite fit all the way around the glass, his toes couldn't quite sit flat on the ground in a regular chair. Even his voice felt small as he said, "Babies do that."

She nodded and walked over to where he sat, standing in front of him, her breasts inches from his face. Her hand was soft as she cupped his chin, stroking his cheek, the smell of her strong at her wrists. "Yes, but men do too. Come with me to my bedroom, and I can show you other things that men do." She turned, her finger lingering for a moment on his face, and walked to the door on the other side of the room, her hips moving from side to side as she walked slowly, deliberately, looking over her shoulder with one eye and beckoning to him. She left the door open after her, but did not turn on a light.

James slid down from the chair, his knees wobbling and his spine tingling. His thoughts were jumbled and confused, like he was thinking in a language he did not yet understand.

Now, there's a good life lesson in all of this. To say it simply: if something's too good to be true, it probably is. To say it in a more complicated, but fitting for the story way: if a witch suddenly disappears and in her place is a gorgeous woman who is trying hard to seduce you, something very bad might be about to happen.

Luckily for James, a moan cut through his mental fog, a low and mournful thing, and he shivered, his steps faltering. In the corner by the cast-iron stove, where there had been nothing just moments before, the outline of the black-haired woman sat. Her hands were bound to the chair, one of them bleeding from a stump of a missing finger, and a piece of cloth was strapped tightly over her mouth. She moaned again at him from behind her gag, her eyes wide and wet, the cloth cutting off all coherent sound and replacing it with that low moan. Her eyes seemed to be pleading with him, begging. Behind him the door to the bedroom stood open, promising him untold delights, and before him sat the black-haired woman. He frowned. Something wasn't right.

With a sharp jerk he peeled away the cloth covering her mouth, unwinding the gag. When her mouth was free she took a deep breath and began to sing.

James had always loved music; he loved sitting in the living room and playing with his mother's old record player, dancing when he was sure no one was watching him. It was one of the few things he had left of her, and he would often spend hours at a time flipping through records from bands he had never heard of. It was a way of getting to know his mother, who had passed some years before. So he knew music, was no stranger to it, but he had never heard music quite like that before.

It was low and sad, haunting even, the notes slowly climbing over one another, scaling and falling. They evoked a surreal mix of emotions within James. At the outset was a sadness; the low and slow notes were mournful, carrying the dignified weight of a eulogy, but they were not sustained. From the terrible lows they grew to dizzying and giddy heights, leaving James with a bittersweet feeling of having lost something he was happy to have had, if only for a time.

Behind him came a low shrieking growl. The crone stood in the doorway, with her gravestone teeth and barren breasts, the same doorway that the beautiful woman had beckoned James through only a few moments before. She snarled at them both and snaked out, catching James on the cheek with her nails, lunging toward him and the singing woman. The tied-down woman could do nothing but sing louder, so sing she did. It had an effect, causing the old crone to shrink back and hold her hands to her ears. Finally, with a poof, she evaporated into little wisps of black smoke, melting into the air.

CHAPTER TWO

Without the cloth over her mouth James was able to get a good look at the woman as he untied her. Her face was quite striking, her hair a dark black river that cascaded over one shoulder. She wore a modest white gown; her skin was a light caramel color, her eyes a woodland green. Where her finger had been bitten off, new bone sprouted even as James watched, muscles growing over it like vines, and finally new skin formed. Before he knew it, she had a complete hand again.

"That's better," she said. "Thank you, my young hero. I'm not sure what would have happened had you not been here to free me."

"I'm James," he said, sticking his hand out, "who are you?"

She dropped to her knees and smiled, offering her own hand in return. A patch of freckles on her nose caught the candlelight, and for some unknown reason they made James indescribably happy. "My name is Jewel. I'm the character of this story."

She held his hand as she led him out of the cottage. Outside the fog had abated and he could see more of their environment. There were trees all around with birds fluttering in them and squirrels rustling up their trunks. The ground felt more solid, his feet didn't sink in as he walked. "So what happened?"

"My original story is about a witch in that cottage, the very same witch, actually, that you helped me defeat."

On the outside, after the witch's defeat, the house didn't seem so frightening. After all, it wasn't the cottage that was bad, just the witch inside. With the fog receding and the sun beginning to shine through, the stonework actually looked somewhat pleasant.

"So are you saying I need to be a part of this story for it to go well?" James asked.

She smiled and stroked the back of his head, turning and leading him back down the path. "No, my song should be enough, but something has been happening here in the stories." Stopping, she took James by the shoulder. "I've done this story thousands of times, I know how it should go, but this last time something changed."

"What happened?" James asked.

"I was at the worst part of my story, right when I was tied up and it looked like the witch would have me for supper. Every other time we did the story it would be at that point that I felt my heart fill with courage and I started to sing my song. Well, right as I was about to do that a man walked in."

"Who was it?"

Her face fell and lines grew around her mouth as she

thought of him. James squeezed her hand, hoping to give her a little bit of courage. "I'd heard rumors about him before. All the stories are connected, you see, and I've got a few that I like to go traveling through. Some of my friends told me of a man whose face never changed, with black pits for eyes and teeth as sharp as razors. They said he was a thing even nightmares are afraid of, and when he smiles at you your insides go numb. I should have believed them." She shivered violently, her skin breaking out in goosebumps. "It makes me feel cold just thinking about it, like it just started snowing in my heart."

"Do you know his name?"

She nodded, her face pale. "Gladhands," she said in a whisper. "He looked just as horrible as the rumors said. When he came near me my voice just vanished, and all these terrible whispers started in my head. It was terrible. He put that tape over my mouth to keep me quiet when he left, kept me from completing my own story, and just left the witch to do what she wanted. Over and over my fingers grew back and she just ate them again, one by one." She rubbed at her arms to try and warm them. "It has been a nightmare."

They reached the spot where he had originally entered the story. Above them the hole up to the office stood. Jewel lifted James up so that he could crawl back through the page; he turned just as he was on the other side. "Will I ever get to see you again?" he asked.

She smiled up at him from her world. "Oh yes, come back anytime you like. I'll be here for you." James pulled his face back and the page was just another sheet of paper, the glow faded, leaving him alone in his father's office.

Daybreak was just beginning to lighten up the sky as James closed the door to the office and tiptoed down the hall. He was in the middle of the stairs heading back to his room, avoiding the fourth stair, which creaked, when he heard the sound of his father in the kitchen.

Their house had an old electric coffee grinder. James' father always described the thing as 'bulletproof,' and swore he would never have to buy another. That was all true, the construction on it was sound, but the thing was as loud as a bulldozer for fifteen seconds every morning. James ignored it and continued up the stairs, but something striking caught his ear in the silence after the grinder. A low hummed version of the song that Jewel had sung was coming from the kitchen. It was the exact same, James was sure of it. He walked back down and peeked in the kitchen door.

His father stood at the counter with an untied bathrobe hanging off his shoulders. Overhanging his red boxer shorts his hairy belly bulged, jiggling as Patrick swayed back and forth. He was humming as he poured himself a cup of coffee, the same song that Jewel had sung, note for note.

"Oh, hey Bud," Patrick said, noticing him at the doorway, "what are you doing up this early?" He sipped at his coffee and a little black dribble slipped out of the corner of his mouth, sliding down the bushy grey beard he had worn since before James could remember.

"I couldn't sleep," he said. "What are you humming?"

His father smiled, eyes far away. "You know, it's a song I haven't thought about in a long time. I woke up with it stuck in my head. Strange how these things work." He took his cup of coffee and walked past James. "Go back to bed. You don't have school for another few hours. You don't want to be tired in class."

He walked up the steps to his bedroom, no longer bothering to be quiet, pondering the mystery of Jewel's song.

"James?" his father's voice followed him up the stairs. "Come back down here, please."

It is a given that every child knows when they are in trouble simply by the tone in their parent's voice, and this was no different. James felt a dash of fear against his insides, his foot hovering an inch off the top step. He turned and walked back down the stairs, butterflies in his stomach. His father was standing at his open office door, his eyebrows contracted. "Have you been in my office?"

James swallowed hard, his mouth suddenly feeling like it was full of sand.

His father walked over to him, looking down from his full height. "Have you been in my office? I don't like asking twice."

When James' voice came it was only a whisper. "I had to..."

His father breathed deeply, the wind whistling through his nostrils, his fingers drumming against the side of his coffee cup. "Do we need to have another conversation about personal boundaries?"

"No sir," James said, tucking his chin down to his chest and staring intently at the floor.

"Look me in the eyes while we're talking," his father said, lifting his chin. "I've told you before, there's a lot of dangerous stuff in there. I don't want you in there when I'm not. Do we understand each other?"

"Yes sir," James said.

His father pointed to the top of the stairs. "Now, get back to bed and get another hour of sleep, then I'll make you some breakfast before school. And remember what I said about personal boundaries. I don't want to have this discussion again."

"Yes sir," James said, his insides twisting among themselves. He took the steps slowly, one at a time, and went back to bed.

CHAPTER THREE

I should probably take a moment to tell you a little about Patrick, James' father. This story is as much about him as it is James. You see, Patrick is one of those guys who believes he holds the world up. You can see it in his shoulders, how he holds them tightly together, hunched over. It's not often that they relax and when they do, you can bet money that scotch is involved.

That is not to say that Patrick is a bad man; far from it. As his wife used to say, he does his sawdust best. He's a fairy tale maker by trade, trafficking in dreams. It was a good job for a man like him, who valued his alone time as much as another man might value gold.

That's enough about Patrick, though you're sure to find out more later, some things good, some things not so good. But for right now we'll get back to the story.

*****

Patrick barely spoke a word to James as they drove along the country roads toward the school. This wasn't a new thing, his father would sometimes go for hours without saying a word, just sitting, wrapped up in his own mind. However, with a man like Patrick there are two types of silences. There was a silence of introspection, and a silence of anger. He wasn't the type of man to tell you he was angry, he would swallow it down and let it simmer for a while. Once there for a few hours, when he had time to taste it and see if it was worth sharing or not, he would either let it go forever or have a painfully methodical discussion about why he was mad. James watched out the window as the forest rolled by, hoping it would all just be let go.

They lived out in the country in a little house that Patrick had built himself. It was a source of pride for him, the fact that he had built it with his own hands. The years that Patrick was working on it were some of the happiest that James could remember. His mother Catherine was still alive then and they all lived in a tiny trailer on the land while Patrick built. Though the trailer was cramped, and often cold, James hadn't minded.

The house was the only one in the middle of a forest, built out of logs and stone pulled from a nearby field. It always looked anachronistic, like it belonged in some other century, but James loved that about it.

As they drove, spears of light shot through cracks in the forest and shined on the windshield. Autumn was coming, though it was not close enough to justify the thick coat Patrick had made James wear; the fire of fall was barely a spark in the leaves.

The coat was too hot, made of a flannel that itched his neck, the tail of it riding high and leaving the small of his back exposed, the sleeves hanging up above his wrists when he moved, forcing him to pull them down every minute or so.

The trees petered off and a golden sea of farmland took over, each field seeming to have a little red house and barn in the middle of it like a spot of blood. The neighbors could say all they wanted about the slant of their roof or the leaks in their pipes, but at least their house didn't look exactly like every other one within a ten-mile radius.

Farmland and amber waves of grain turned to speckled little white houses sharing their yards with one another, the proximity of them getting closer and closer together as they entered the town. Patrick rolled through stop signs, never coming to a full stop. With each tap the wheels squealed a high pitch of protest before the car slowed. Finally they parked before an orange brick building with brown trim, James ducking his head as his classmates turned toward the sound of the failing brakes.

"Here you are, Bud, have a good day at school," his father said as James stepped out of the car. Students were funneling in the front door to the school. A man in a suit stood held the door open for them. James listened to the rattle and squeal of the car as it drove off behind him, hoping no one was paying too close attention.

"Good morning, Mr. Jenkins," James said to the mustachioed middle-aged man holding the door open.

"Good morning to you, James," the man replied. "I'll see you in class. You run along now."

*****

His locker, lucky number 113, opened on the second time he tried his lock. Perhaps he just wasn't good at the fine movements opening a school lock required, but it always seemed like the thing thwarted him purposefully. He never got it open on the first try. When he did there were printed out pictures of beautiful women hung on the inside of the door. His friend Mitchell had been the first to do that in his grade; he had been the second, cutting out women at random from an old People magazine the library had.

"Hey shit-licker," a voice called out as he was gathering his books. James didn't have to look to know whose voice it was, and his stomach had an immediate sinking sensation. Kenny Halvorford.

Kenny was a big kid, a good five or six inches taller than James, and thick too. Mitchell and James called him fat whenever he wasn't around, but there was muscle there too. Enough to get put on the line for the school's football team. James had watched a game or two from the sidelines, and been bored out of his mind. The quarterback only had enough arm strength to throw the ball underhanded a few yards, but Kenny took his job of pushing down the other kids seriously. Every school had a kid like Kenny, a boy who grew just a little faster than everyone else and fashioned himself king of the place because of it.

Kenny leaned up against the lockers next to James, mouth-breathing into his face. Kids like that always had a particular smell about them, like a combination of sweat, sour milk and whatever they had for breakfast. That day it smelled like eggs.

"Your dad done it, yet?" Kenny said.

James stacked his books under his arm and slipped a pencil into his jeans. "No, and it's not going to happen. It was just a one-time thing, is all. The counselor said it happens more often than you'd think." He shut his locker and walked away from Kenny. Some days it was just better to leave it alone.

A thick hand spun him around. Kenny brushed his blonde hair out of his eyes and puffed out his chest. It was apparent that he didn't want to let James drop it. "Not to normal people.

My dad told me about it. Said he had to call in a *per-fesh-in-aw* to talk to your dad."

"Pro," another voice called out. Mitchell came down the hall, a thick textbook held in his hand. Mitchell was bigger than James, but not as large as Kenny. He played on the soccer team, his legs thick, his black hair cropped short. "It's professional. Don't say words you don't know, Kenny, it makes you sound like an idiot."

"What, does James have to call in backup every time I try to talk to him?" Kenny said. "You guys go play with each others' shits. I'm off to class."

"He really needs to stop using that word," Mitchell said. "Don't pay any attention to what he said about your dad. He's just being a jerk. Guys like that aren't worth it."

A bell echoed down the halls of the school. "Yeah. Hey, I got to get to class," James said. "I'll see you later." He walked down the length of the rapidly emptying hallway toward Mr. Jenkins' classroom.

Just outside the door a rank smell stopped him in his tracks. It smelled of rotting eggs and horse manure and something else, something indescribable. There was no one near James, and he checked the soles of his shoes to make sure he hadn't stepped in anything. The hall was empty and clean. The smell disappeared and he shrugged it off, taking his seat by the window as Mr. Jenkins began his lesson.

Jenkins was a good teacher, but he had been cursed with an inability to enunciate. It wasn't that the things he said weren't important, or interesting, but he spoke every sentence in a monotone. Each syllable sounded exactly like the last, and soon James' eyes were wandering toward the window. He was not the only one, either. Kyle, the kid who sat in front of him and was known for infrequent bathing, also turned his head to the window as soon as the lecture started.

There are few things more distracting to a child in school than an open window. It tantalized James with the cool fall breeze, the lush playground just visible in the corner. The bars of the jungle gym seemed to be calling to him, telling him he needed to be out there climbing their heights, hanging by his legs underneath them. Even the tree looked like it was gesturing to him, waving him over, wanting nothing more than a child to sit under its shade.

He sat bolt upright in his chair. Having been in school a month, he had been staring at that tree for a month. He knew that tree, knew the knobs and the wisps of its wood. Knew every branch and root, and as he sat in class he was sure that something had changed.

The trunk bulged and grew as he watched. He gasped as he realized that it was not that the tree was *changing*, but rather that there was something right behind the tree *moving*. The bulge turned into a foot, the foot into a leg, and soon a hulking ogre stepped out from behind the tree.

James' eyes widened and he looked around at his classmates beside him. Most of them were sitting glass-eyed as Mr. Jenkins read from a book while drawing figures on the chalkboard. Even those, like James, who were looking out the window had looks of complete boredom. It was apparent that no one else could see what he could.

The figure was tall, almost half the height of the tree, colored a forest green with black streaks of soot all over him. Steam came off his bald head, the only hair was a few curled and singed strands. His skin was peeling off in places and weeping green blood. Still, his muscles were fearsome and the club that he dragged looked very real and very painful. The thing stared at James, a layer of drool falling out his open mouth and down onto his hairy chest, not moving, simply looking. The eyes burned like dying embers as he watched, and waited.

"James, do you know the answer?" Mr. Jenkins asked, causing James to jump and tear his eyes from the ogre.

His mouth fell open and the class stared at him. "I'm sorry," he said, "I didn't catch what the question was."

Mr. Jenkins frowned at him, pulling at the sides of his

mustache, disappointment etched in his brow. "Why don't you pay attention to what's going on up here? Okay?"

"Yes sir," James said, giving a cursory glance back to the tree. The thing was no longer standing there, he was nowhere within sight of the window. The tree looked just as it had when he first sat down.

"Watch him closely, sir," Kenny said from the other side of the room, "I hear crazy runs in the family. You never know what he's thinking."

A red flush burned James' cheeks and he put his head down, avoiding eye contact with any other students. He suddenly became very interested in the little doodle he was tracing in his notebook.

It was a rare student that could get a rise out of Montgomery Jenkins, but Kenny Halvorford was certainly not the norm. "Hey!" Mr. Jenkins barked, storming over to Kenny's desk and lifting him bodily by the arm. "I've told you before to knock that talk off. Now if you can't do it, I don't want you in my class. Report to the office." He dragged the child to the door and pushed him out of it, slamming it shut after him.

Normally Mr. Jenkins was one of the understanding teachers. He may not have been the most charismatic, but he always seemed to remember what it was like to be James' age. However, on that day he did the one thing that James was silently pleading with him not to do. The teacher strode up next to his desk, knelt down, and put a hand on his shoulder. "You okay, James?" he asked in a quiet voice that everyone heard.

James twisted his own wrists under the desk to keep from crying. It was already bad enough. He had felt their hot stares on him to see if Kenny was right, see if it really did run in the family, see if he was about to do something *kuhrazy*. Why did Mr. Jenkins have to make it worse by calling attention to it? "I'm fine," he said in a hurried tone. He could feel his shoulders pull up toward his body, the tension building. If only they would all stop *looking* at him!

"You know," Mr. Jenkins continued, "if you ever need someone to talk about what happened, my door is always open."

"I said I'm *fine*," James hissed through clenched teeth.

Finally Mr. Jenkins nodded and went back to the front of the class. James had never felt so thankful to hear the man's dull monotone. He kept his head down for the rest of the class until the bell rang. When it did, he was the first out the door, not saying a word to anyone, wanting to forget the Kenny Halvorfords and the Mr. Jenkins of the world.

Unfortunately, Kenny was waiting for him by his locker.

CHAPTER FOUR

James' stomach tightened, and he was unable to distinguish whether it was fear or anger that caused it. Kenny leaned against the locker next to his, his arms crossed in a stance of nonchalance.

While trying to keep his hands from shaking, James avoided eye contact with Kenny. Bullies were like bees in that regard; you had to do your best not to show fear. James liked thinking of Kenny in that way, like an irritating little bee he just had to ignore.

"We're not always going to have teachers around, you know," Kenny buzzed in a low voice. "And you're not always going to have Mitchell to fight your fights, you little shit-heel."

James put away his notebook and grabbed his folder for English. His hands were trembling and his jaw was sore with how hard he was grinding his teeth.

Kenny chewed on his nails thoughtfully, spitting them out on James' feet. "You know, my dad thinks your dad never would have done it, so you don't really have to worry. Dad said he did it for the attention; your dad hadn't sold any of his faggy-tales in a while and needed the money." Kenny stuck a hand in James' locker and fingered his coat. "Look at this piece of shit! I knew you were poor, but I didn't realize you had to go digging in the garbage for clothes. Tell you what, come by my place and I'll give you my shitty old clothes."

"Shut up!" James yelled and he grabbed his locker door with both hands, swinging it shut as hard as he could, catching the fingers on Kenny's right hand in between the locker and frame.

The hallway fell silent as Kenny howled in pain, his voice elevating several octaves. His fingers immediately turned a dark shade of purple where the locker had hit him. Tears sprang out freely and fell down his flushed cheeks.

James felt two things at that moment, an intense feeling of self-satisfaction, and an incredible fear about what his punishment would be. Not wanting to stick around to find out, James turned to run. Unfortunately for him the janitor grabbed him by the seat of his pants and held him back, keeping him at the scene of the crime. Teachers appeared seemingly out of nowhere to surround them, some looking at Kenny's swelling hand, others helping the janitor hold James.

The next few minutes were mostly a blur for him. He was dragged down the hallway and planted in the chair outside the principal's office. His stomach flipped and flopped around inside of him while he waited. Was he sorry for what he had done? On some level he felt like he should be, knowing that wrong was wrong, but on a different level, a more primal and savage level, he had gotten a secret thrill at exacting his own brand of justice.

The thrill was extremely short lived, however, and died completely when he heard the secretary call home to his father. When he was finally ushered into the principal's office, his legs were watery and shook with each step.

Principal Waters was a tall, thin man with a pair of thick orange glasses and a pencil thin mustache. He liked to lean over his desk and let the glasses slide down his nose, giving him a look of gradual severity; the longer the conversation, the more severe he looked.

"James, your father is on the way to pick you up, but before he gets here I thought we could take a chance to talk," Principal Waters said, folding his hands together in a pyramid.

"Kenny deserved it. He's always bullying me," James said.

"I don't want to talk about Mr. Halvorford. We've had our share of problems with him. What I want to talk about is you. How have you been feeling lately?"

James sat back and crossed his arms over his chest. He had never been sent to the principal's office before, but from what he had heard from Mitchell, Waters just yelled at you for what you did wrong. He hadn't been expecting this. "Why do you care?"

Waters sat back in his chair. "It's a small town; we all have to take care of each other. Your family's had a rough couple of years. We all know that. It would be natural for you to have some confusing feelings that you need to work out. I'm just trying to help, so let me ask you again, how have you been feeling lately?"

"I've been feeling irritated that everyone keeps asking me that question," James said, sliding down in his chair, his chin lowering to his chest.

"Well, I can see you don't really want to talk to me, and that's fine. But I want you to know, it's a lot for anyone to handle, so if you ever need to talk about it you can come to me. Now, I do have to administer some sort of punishment for shutting your locker door on Kenny's fingers. You're very lucky that he didn't break one of them, and no matter what you're going through, that's never acceptable. If Kenny is doing something to you, you need to come to us and tell us about it. So I think we'll send you home today, and the next three days you'll be in detention during lunch time."

There was a knock at the door and then his father was standing in the doorway. Patrick was wearing a flannel shirt and a pair of jeans with ink stains around the pockets, his mouth held in a frown, the tip of his salt and pepper beard quivering. "Let's go, young man," he said, motioning toward the door.

"Patrick, may I have a word with you in private?" Waters asked as James was exiting the door.

"Sure," Patrick said before turning to his son. "Just wait outside, Bud, I'll be out in a minute."

James sat back down on the chair and tried to listen to the muffled conversation that they were having. He could hear almost nothing. They were talking in a hushed whisper, but when his father came out he was very pale.

They didn't say a word to each other until they were seated in the car. Patrick lifted a hand to start the car, seemed to change his mind, and then sat back, leaving the keys in the column. His lips were pursed and he wouldn't look at his son. "What did Kenny say to you?" he asked, his voice quiet.

James swallowed hard, his throat feeling thick. "It doesn't matter. Can we just go home?"

"It does matter, James," Patrick said. "It matters very much. Tell me what he said."

"He said you did it for attention," James said after a moment.

Kenny's father had used a phrase after the car took his dad away that night, a clinical and sterile phrase that James would remember the sound of forever. He could barely think it, the only way was to break it up into syllables. *Ah-temp-tad-sew-es-eyed.*

Patrick sat back in the seat and seemed to deflate, the air whooshing out of him, the smell of his coffee breath filling the car. If anything, he got paler. "I made a mistake once. There's a kind of...fog that gets in me sometimes. I'm sorry that you're having to deal with some fallout because of that. My problems shouldn't be anyone's but my own." He turned in his seat, holding a finger up to James' nose. "But don't you think for one minute that that gives you an excuse to physically harm another human being. I don't care what he says about me, you're better than that. Now, let's get you home. You're grounded for the next three weeks."

They drove home in silence, the only noise being the squeal of the brakes and the shake of the front tires as Patrick passed over bumps in the road.

CHAPTER FIVE

James had originally been sentenced to go immediately to bed without any dinner, but after a few hours his father relented, poking his head in to the room with a bowl of tomato soup and a grilled ham-and-cheese sandwich. He sat in bed reading; there was no television nor computer allowed in his room, though his father had never once deprived him of access to any book he wanted. He fell asleep with his copy of The Hobbit tented on his chest.

It was the smell that woke him later that night. The smell of burned flesh and burned hair, that sickly sweet bacon-that's-gone-bad smell. It wrinkled his nose and he sat up in bed, his eyes crusty with sleep. Though he was just about to turn over and try to ignore the smell until he fell asleep, his door swung open and something large stepped inside.

An immobilizing fear gripped him; he felt like his stomach had just fallen out the bottom of him and scurried under the bed. Standing over him, hunched in the room, was the ogre that he had seen on the playground earlier.

With his face so close, James could see every hair and scar. The lips were missing, the teeth were sharp and dripping sour-smelling saliva down onto his bedspread, the eyes yellowed and uneven, one larger than the other. There were blackened patches of skin that bubbled up with pus; he looked to have been burned horrendously. The ogre lifted his mammoth hand and grasped the front of James' red pajamas, his claws digging into the fabric easily.

"Jewel said to find you, that you would help," the ogre said in a voice that was surprisingly eloquent and melodious.

James eyed the ogre warily. The thing didn't exactly look trustworthy. Of course, aside from breaking into James' room in the dead of night, he hadn't exactly done anything to warrant such a condemnation. Still, there were times for open-mindedness, and James wasn't exactly sure that this was one of them. "Jewel? You mean the pretty dark-haired lady?"

The ogre nodded. "With the beautiful voice. We visit each other's stories from time to time. She saw the trouble I've been having with mine and suggested I bring you there. She's just a few stories over."

"What's the trouble?" James asked.

The ogre let go of James and sat down on the end of his bed, causing it to groan and creak alarmingly. "I'm not an ogre. Everyone calls me that but I'm not. Name's Ryan. I'm actually a shepherd. Oh sure, it's nothing glamorous like being a prince or a knight, but I like what I do. I work the fields with my son." He held up a hand and turned to James. "You see, early in my story I run into a witch. She's pretty standard as far as fairy tales go, got the warts on her nose and everything." He paused and scratched at his singed eyebrow. "Hates toads, though, so I guess she breaks the mold a little bit. I wronged her by not taking her in one night when it was cold. I know, I know, not the most neighborly thing in the world, but I got a kid, you know? I have to be looking out for his safety. Well, next thing I know I'm cursed to look like this until the end of time." The ogre cocked an eye at James. "Witches really can be temperamental. Best to stay away from them all together, if you can."

James wiped some of the crust from his eyes. "So you need me to take care of the witch for you? All I did in the other story was to take the gag off Jewel; she took care of her witch herself. I don't have an innate witch-fighting ability if that's what you're thinking."

The ogre wiped a bit of drool off his chin onto the corner of James' blanket. "Sorry, when I'm like this I tend to salivate quite heavily. I think it's the smell of the cat, something about this form makes me crave it. But about the witch, no. Not at all. The witch is actually pretty integral to the story. She turns me into the ogre and then I go running through the town, trying to get someone to help me. Instead of helping me, the people of the town form an angry mob to tie me up and try to burn me at the stake. It's all meant to instruct; I didn't help, so no one will help me and all that."

"You turning into an ogre is in the story?" James asked.

"It *is* the story. Without any of that happening, I wouldn't have a reason to exist, and I would just disappear. No one wants to read a story where nothing happens and everyone lives in harmony. That's boring, there's nothing to learn or experience there."

"So what's supposed to happen when they try to burn you at the stake?" James asked.

The ogre smiled, as much as his deformed face would allow him to, his eyes suddenly soft and brimming with tears. "Leo. My son, he joins the crowd and hears me speak, hears me plead, and he recognizes that it's me. I'm tied to the stake by this point, just surrounded by kindling, the fire beginning to burn, and he jumps right in there with me." The ogre paused for a moment, wiping away a tear. "I'm sorry, I just love that part of the story. He tells them that it's me, that my outsides may have changed but it was still me down deep, and he unties me. That's what's *supposed* to happen anyway."

"What changed?" James asked.

The ogre turned to him, suddenly quiet and somber. "The man in the suit came. I don't know much about him. I saw him take Leo off somewhere, and things just ground to a halt.

47

He wore black and white, tall, but I couldn't see a single feature on his face. The crowd was too thick in front of him." Lines of worry crested the green and black charred face. "I don't know where my Leo is, but he's not saving me, so I'm stuck burning." The ogre grabbed James by the shoulder painfully hard. "I don't care about the burning, but you've got to get my Leo back! I need to know he's okay!"

James put both of his hands up in the air in front of him. "I'm sorry mister, but I don't know what I can do to help you. I'm grounded for the next few weeks, and I'm not exactly sure how to beat this suit guy. I really think that you might want to find someone else for the job."

What else could you really expect from James? Helping Jewel was one thing, but an ogre? And besides, it was a school night and he was already in a lot of trouble with his father. Thank you very much but he had to decline.

Ryan, the ogre, sat with his head in his hands for a few moments. He scratched at his chin, his mismatched eyes staring out James' window. For a moment James actually felt bad for the guy. He had traveled all the way into the real world just to get shot down by some kid in his pajamas.

"You know what?" Ryan said, holding out one finger. "There's something I forgot. You'll have to forgive me, but being in this form makes me start to think like an ogre."

James put on hand onto the hulk's shoulder and patted it kindly. "It's no problem, what did you forget?"

The ogre turned and leered at James. "I'm a lot bigger than you." Before James could react, the ogre grabbed him around the midsection with one massive hand and dragged him out of the room. Though he looked monstrously tall and wide, the ogre seemed to be able to contort his way through the doorways and down the stairs to his father's office with ease. The door was ajar at the end of it, a glowing blue light coming from the crack.

Once again a window had opened up on the stack of pages on top of his father's desk. James struggled, kicking his legs into the side of the ogre, but it had no affect. He wasn't even sure if the monster felt him. The ogre stepped in through the pages, dragging James down with him.

CHAPTER SIX

When he met the ground it was with a thump and a whoosh, all the air driven from his body in the rib-bruising fall. While getting to his feet he tried to take stock of his surroundings. There was fog all around him, leaving everything beyond ten feet a blur. He was in some sort of field, uncut grass underfoot, and distant sounds of a commotion were in the air.

"What's with the fairy-tale land and fog?" he said aloud. Turning his head each way, he realized he was alone, the ogre no longer beside him. Above him the page stayed open, and he seriously considered just climbing back out of the place. Unfortunately for James, it was a few feet out of reach, and he would have to get some sort of ladder in order to return.

Off in the distance a flame flickered to life, and then several more just to the side of it. There was a slight tremor in the very base of James' stomach, a sourness that made him want to simply sit down and wait the story out, but he knew he wouldn't. His mind and his gut were going in two very different directions. He stepped cautiously in the direction of the light.

As he made his way across the hard ground, the fog thinned and the commotion grew louder. Soon James was able to see a group of men and women, mostly dressed in simple spun clothes, holding lit torches and circled around a bundle that they had tied on a platform. A drunk at the back of the crowd swayed visibly when James walked by him, shaking his bottle and mumbling something incoherent.

When he got close enough he could see the platform that they were all surrounding. It wasn't a platform at all, but rather a gigantic wagon with rocks jammed under the wheels to keep it steady. Through the middle a pole as thick as a tree was mounted, at the base of which the ogre sat tied with thick strands of rope. His chin was touching his chest, his eyes closed, drool running freely out of his mouth. There were no burns nor scorch marks on him.

A man jumped on top of the wagon and waved his hands for silence. He was a stocky fellow, covered in thick furs, a sword belted onto his back, with a ragged beard growing down his face in braided strands. The crowd quieted quickly.

"My friends and neighbors, we need to make a decision for what we are to do with the monster now that we've caught it. We can't just sit around here yelling at it all day. It'll get out eventually. When my band of warriors found it we gave it more than a few good lumps to the head, but we don't know exactly what it'll take to kill this thing. It was a frightful fight just to get it like this."

"What did he do to you?" James shouted out. Though his small voice was somewhat lost in the noise, it caught the attention of the man on the platform. James passed easily through the legs of the onlookers and stood at the base of the platform.

The warrior stared down his bushy eyebrows at James, his head cocked to the side as though he couldn't fathom how a person could even ask such a question. "It's been terrorizing us for years! Every unexplained death, all the livestock that's went missing these last few years, it must have been this ogre, can't you see that?" The rest of the crowd shouted in agreement.

James cocked a skeptical eyebrow at the man, his neck beginning to get sore from having to look up at him at such an extreme angle. He crossed his arms over his chest. "Do you *know* that it was him? I mean, when did you guys first *see* this ogre?"

"I was the one to see it first," a plump young woman shouted out, her voice high pitched and grating. "I saw it two nights ago. It was walking behind my chicken coop, coming out from the witch's forest. Only evil comes out of that forest." She looked very pleased with herself, smiling around with a goofy grin on her face.

"Okay," James said, spreading his arms. He spoke in the deliberately slow way some adults spoke to children. "So the first you saw of him was two days ago. Yet you're attributing to him every bad thing from the last few *years*. Don't you think that you might just be trying to make this man into a scapegoat?"

"It's not a goat, it's an ogre," the plump woman yelled out, to the accompanying cheers of the crowd.

James crawled his way up the large wagon wheel and stood next to the warrior and the ogre. If Leo wouldn't be here to give the speech to free the ogre, James would gladly take that responsibility. He stood for a moment with his mouth slightly agape, thinking of what he could say to convince these people of the ogre's humanity. "Listen, I know that this seems like an easy answer to your problems, but the easy answers aren't always right. You see, this isn't an ogre at all, it's a member of your community who got turned into a monster." He turned and reached for the ropes to untie the bound ogre. "So why don't we just untie him and all go back home?"

A flash of light and sudden pain rocked him to the side, throwing him down onto the wooden planks of the wagon. For a moment he saw two of everything, two ogres, two crowds, two warriors standing over him. Then the two became one and he realized that the warrior had hit him and was now standing over him with his sword drawn.

"This one's in league with the ogre!" the warrior shouted.

"He can't be trusted, he spins lies to free it so it can eat us all!"

*****

Now, this is a good teaching moment. There are some things in the world that won't listen to reason, no matter what, and you're better off not trying. A nest of wasps, for example. No matter how calmly you try to explain that it was not you who disturbed them, they won't listen, and you will have lost all that valuable time to run away. Angry mobs are like that; they won't listen to reason and most times you're better off just getting out of the way. But I digress.

*****

The crowd began its jeering again, closing in on James with their torches raised. In the firelight they looked less like people, their eyes darkened to shadows, their teeth glistening and glowing with an orange light. James stood up hesitantly, very conscious of the sharp blade pointed at him. It was a bad spot for him to be in.

Luckily for James the wagon shuddered jarringly under him and the creak of wood and ropes sounded through the air. The ogre stirred, every movement of his gargantuan body shifting

54

the wagon. Though he was tied with the thickest of ropes that the town could find, the ogre struggled against them, growling and gnashing his teeth toward the crowd. Every eye was on the wood and the ropes, James himself wondered whether they would hold. His wonder was overpowered by his instinct for self-preservation and he took the valuable time that the ogre had created for him and ran off.

The crowd, distracted by their fear of the awakened ogre, did not notice a young boy darting between their legs. James was able to make it beyond their circle when he heard them begin to shout. "Fire! Fire! Grab kindling quickly, we'll burn it with fire!"

*****

James couldn't see what help he could be in the town, and if truth be told he was more than a little afraid of the crowd. He had misjudged them, had thought that a few simple sentences would be enough to sway them. He ran headlong into the fog that surrounded the town, not really thinking at all, just wanting to be out of reach of those bloodthirsty creatures. After he was sure he was safe he could worry about where Leo was.

Soon he was lost, beyond the glow of the torches, surrounded by the thick fog, running aimlessly until at last he came upon a wall of trees. They were tall, dark, and leafless, their ends sticking out like hands. There was an opening in front of him, a dark path into the woods. It all seemed terribly familiar.

Though the woods wasn't pitch dark, James still felt his way along the path gingerly, his hands gliding from tree to tree, the moss that grew on them slimy under his touch. Soon he came upon a cottage, a small cabin in the woods made of stone. A tremor of trepidation thrummed through the very bottom of his stomach. He had not had much luck with cottages out in the woods, but if the path lead there, then clearly there was something important about it. Everything has a purpose in a story, though for good or ill James had no clue.

He walked up to the door and raised his hand, about to knock, when it opened from the inside and a small woman appeared.

"Yeah?" she said, looking up at him. Though James was short for his age, the woman was even shorter, hunched over a cane, her nose crooked and spotted with warts. "What do you want? You're not asking for money, are you? Because I live in a swamp, so clearly I don't have much."

"No, ma'am, actually I came about Ryan, the ogre," James said.

The small woman sneered at him and knocked him sharply

on the knees with her cane. "No take backs! He failed his test, so I get to curse him. Only pure love and understanding will free him. That's how it works, I won't change it."

James rubbed gingerly at his knee, nursing a bruise. For as small a woman as she was, she had surprising strength. "So that's who you are. No, it's not about that. Apparently that's all supposed to happen in the story, and he's fine with that. It's his kid, actually. Leo. I'm trying to find him so he can do his part of the story. Do you know where he is?"

She sucked at her teeth, making a squelching noise, eying him up. Finally she turned back to her cottage and held the door open for him. "Well, why don't you come inside. I got a kettle on the stove, about to make myself a bit of earl grey. Come on in."

He followed her inside the cottage, limping slightly. The ceiling was very low. James had to duck to avoid hitting his head, and every chair looked too small and frail for his body. He decided to sit on the floor, putting him at about eye level with the witch.

"So why come to my cabin? Why would you assume I know where the boy is? You got something against witches? Because that sort of bigotry won't get you anywhere in the world."

James looked toward the door. Every minute that passed seemed like a precious gem being lost. For all he knew, Ryan could be suffering already. "I'm sorry to rush you, but the ogre is about to be burned. I really need to find Leo if we have any chance of putting this story right."

The witch waved her knobbly hand and poured two cups of tea. "Nah, don't worry about it. Time is funny in a story, I'm sure you'll have just enough of it and not a minute more. Now, why would you assume I know where the boy is? Because yes, us witches can get a bad rap, but there's good and bad ones of us, just like everything else in the world."

"I didn't know whether you'd know or not. I just ran into the woods and saw your cabin. You're the first human in this story I've encountered since the mob."

The witch cackled to herself. "All paths through the woods lead to the witch's cabin, eh? It's a wonder I don't get more visitors." She handed him a steaming cup of tea and took a sip of her own. "It's a bit tart. The creator gave me all the standard witches crap, eye of newt, crow's legs, bat's blood, but do you think he could be bothered to give me a little sugar? I had to get Jewel to bring me the box of tea from a bazaar three stories away for devil's sake."

"The creator?" James asked. "And how do you know Jewel?"

She waved her hand distractedly. "Everybody knows Jewel. As for the creator, you know, I mean whoever wrote this hackneyed story. I've been to some of the other tales," she turned to him, "the one about the mouse warrior? Now that's a story. I mean, I get it, don't get me wrong. This story has a nice moral to it, a good message for the little kiddies, but I think we're one of his earlier attempts. I mean, look how stereotypical he made me!" She spread her arms and twirled before him. "The warty nose, the black shawl, this cottage, it really couldn't get much more stereotypical. I mean, when I think about the sexy witch in Jewel's story," she smiled and shivered, "oof, he should have made me that witch. I would have made a *great* sexy witch."

James did his best to smile and nod back at her. "Do you know where Leo is? Do you have any idea?"

The witch sighed and took another drink of her tea. "Well, I do know that something changed in the story, I felt it shift, though I might be the only one. I'm a little more complex than some of the other characters in this town. I'd check at Leo's home. That's where I felt the change."

In his haste he swallowed the last few gulps of tea and singed his throat. "Do you know how I get there?"

"It should be right next to the bell tower, but I'd be careful there." She put a hand out and touched his, her skin felt paper thin. Though it made him tremble to be touched by her, he made an effort not to pull away. Her eyes were large and watery, a sudden earnestness there. "I'm serious. Something very strange changed there."

James thanked her and set down his tea. "Thanks for your help. I should probably be getting there."

She walked him to her door and gave him a little smile. "I hope it works out for you. I sort of like the end of this story, when Ryan and Leo hug each other. I'd like to see it again."

A shiver ran down James' spine at the sad tone in her voice and he waved goodbye to her, walking back down the path he came from. He took his steps carefully. The mob off in the distance had gathered a sizable amount of wood underneath the ogre and were taking turns holding their torches under his feet. For each time they did it he let out a shriek of pain, howling into the night, and the crowd around him giggled and laughed. If James could help it, he didn't want to catch their attention at all.

It may have been just a trick of the light, but James would swear that they were physically changing from peasants into something else. The spaces where their eyes should be darkened into hollow sockets, their mouths were gaping and toothy, their fingers long and spindly. Even their laughs frightened him. It was no longer a human noise, it was a cackle and howl of otherworldly delight.

The village houses were little more than clay huts, two- or three-room places packed together in the mud and grass of the field. Aside from the witch, everyone else in the story was at the burning, and James didn't run across anyone as he snuck between houses toward the bell tower.

Ryan and Leo's house stood right next to the tower. There was a light flickering in a window and the door was unlocked. James let himself in, though he was careful to look around and make sure no one was following him.

The dimensions inside the hut expanded like a fun house. Though not much more than twenty feet long on the outside, once inside the door James found himself in a hallway that spanned hundreds of feet. The material was different, too, having changed from the wood and straw construction of the hut to a damp stone tunnel, black except for specks of light where torches sat mounted to the wall.

James stepped inside and the door slammed closed behind him. It was paralyzingly cold; his breath came out in a fog. Something soft brushed his ankle and he jumped as a rat the size of a small house cat scurried through a hole in the wall. Spiderwebs rounded the corners of the cieling with spiders as large as James' fist sitting inside them, waiting.

A normal person would have run from that tunnel; there were too many things that bump in the night. But I've said it before and I'll say it again, our James is made from sterner stuff. He felt the fear like anyone would, but he brushed it aside, shoving it into the littlest box in the darkest corner of his mind. One step at a time, he forced his feet forward.

He came upon a bolted-shut wooden door and pressed his ear against it. A frantic muttering came through the wood, though he couldn't make out exactly what it was that was being said. James slid the heavy iron bolt back and the door swung out with a loud creak from the rusted hinges. A gust of air blew out, bringing the sharp sour smell of urine and a metallic coppery scent that he couldn't quite identify. His nose crinkled against it.

Inside was a simple cell, four walls and a cot with some straw on it, and a figure hunched over with his back facing James. "Mr. Gladhands?" a voice whispered out, "Is that you?"

James walked around to the front of the figure and his mouth dropped open. Sitting with his arms bound tightly in a dirty straightjacket was the scariest looking clown that James had ever seen. The smile was red, painted on, as was the nose, and the eyes were a bright shade of blue; all the color was smeared from a trail of dried tears coming from its eyes. Below the straightjacket, where there should have been two healthy looking legs, instead were two mangled and bloody stumps at the end of a pair of bright green pants stained red. His feet were missing beyond the shin, and with every movement a new trickle of blood came out of him.

"Mr. Gladhands?" the clown said again, his voice small and high pitched. "I'll be good, you don't have to take any more of me. I promise I'll be good. Put me back in my own story. I'll be good." The clown writhed in place, falling onto his back, smearing himself with more blood from his stumps, and when he finally rotated around enough to see James, he smiled, his teeth grey and cracked. "Look how good I am!"

James stumbled back out of the room and slammed the door shut, throwing the bolt to lock the door. His knees quivered and he put a hand against the wall to keep himself from falling down. The horror of it was unimaginable.

When the adrenaline finally slowed in his veins, questions began to arise. What was a clown doing in that story? The ogre tale seemed to be fantasy oriented, so where did the clown fit in? Was it bleeding in from stories around them, or had it been brought there and left? James shuddered; he didn't want to think about it. After a moment of hard breathing he gathered his courage to keep walking down the hallway.

Further down there was another door, identical to the previous. Having experienced horror almost too great for his young mind to handle, he thought long and hard about opening the second door.

Though he would not learn of the theory until much later in life, that door was somewhat of a Schrödinger's cat situation.

Inside could be anything, and all the worst possibilities ran through his mind. He put his ear to the door, trying to find out as much about what was inside as possible.

A quiet sniffle came through.

Steeling his resolve, he jerked open the door, covering his eyes and looking through a crack in his fingers. The cell was much the same as the other (*I'll be good!*), except there was a small child, a few years younger than James, hugging his knees and shivering. He had blonde hair cut in the shape of a bowl, and dirt on his face and clothes.

"Leo?" James asked.

The child looked up, his face wet with tears. "This isn't right," he said. "This isn't how the story goes."

James knelt, placing a hand upon the shivering child's back. Leo's arms were so thin James could see the outline of his bones. "How long have you been here?" he asked.

The child looked up to him, his eye sockets deep with shadows. "I don't know. Forever, or maybe just a few minutes. It's wrong, this isn't how it goes. He came and took me. I had to go somewhere but he came and took me. He seemed so nice on the outside." Leo grabbed James' arm with an unexpected forcefulness. "Don't look under his mask, it's hungry."

James picked the child up to his feet. "We have to go, we have to get you out of here." They went to the door and

64

opened it, stepping out into the hall. Leo's eyes opened wide, staring behind James, and his mouth dropped in a silent scream.

Far down at the end of the hallway a torch suddenly snuffed out. As they watched, another torch died, a little closer. As James peered down the hallway he saw that the darkness was not following where the torches had snuffed out; it was advancing steadily. As it passed a third torch, that too was extinguished. The darkness came steadily forward, blowing cold air toward them.

Leo's nails dug into James' arm. "He's here," he whispered.

"Leo, run. Run and save your dad, I'll try to stall whatever is here," James said, turning to face the darkness. His skin tightened in little goose bumps and the hair on the back of his neck stood up.

The little child ran in the other direction, toward the exit. The cold intensified to an extreme, to the point where it hurt James to take a breath and the tips of his fingers began to go numb. James heard the sound of a door slamming shut and knew that Leo was safe.

Out of the silence came the slow and sharp ringing of footsteps. A man walked out of the void, or rather, an approximation of one.

CHAPTER SEVEN

He wore a black and white suit, clean, neatly pressed; his hands were covered in soft-looking white gloves. He was a tall and slender man, and he left one hand in his pocket as he came to a rest before James. Though there was a lot strange about this entire hallway, James found he could not take his eyes from the man's face. The eyes were hollow orbs, the skin around them stretching as though being sucked into that void, the nose was missing completely, he simply had two holes where it should be, and his mouth was smiling hugely, triangular and sharp. There were clasps at the sides of the face, metal shining things that hooked into the skin, and James understood that all this was a mask. Around the sides of it greasy strands of long, black hair fell down around his shoulders.

"Hello, James. My name is Gladhands. I'm very pleased to finally meet you," the man said and he stuck out a gloved hand. It was such an odd formality; James looked wide-eyed at the glove before him. Every instinct in his body told him to run, but he found his legs firmly rooted to the ground. "Shake my hand, James. It's only polite. One must keep up appearances."

Slowly, as though in a dream, James stuck out a hand and

Gladhands seized it, holding it firmly in his own. The hand was thin and boney, but with a ferocious strength. Something wriggled in the palm under the glove, tickling James. "How do you know me?" he asked.

Gladhands finally let go of James' hand. "Your father and I are getting to know each other quite well. You seem to take up a rather large portion of his insides."

"Why did you change Jewel's and the ogre's stories?" James asked.

The mask moved just like a face would, and Gladhands ran a tongue along his row of slimy and sharp teeth before resuming that sharp, triangular smile of his. It was fascinating, in a horrible sort of way, to watch the machinations of his movement. "Not one for small talk, are you? What else do I expect from a child? In the simplest terms, I didn't like their endings. Your father is capable of such wondrous things, and he wastes it on lies. But this is changing, your father is coming to understand that happy endings don't exist."

James took a step back. A twitter of fear, like a small nest of hornets, turned his stomach sour. "What is it you want?"

Gladhands took a step forward. His head tilted, those empty holes boring into James. "To eat," he said.

An electric jolt of energy ran through James and he leaped backwards, turning and sprinting down the hallway as fast as his legs would take him. He never turned his head, but down the entire length of the hallway he could hear Gladhands' steps right behind him. The hairs on his neck stood on end as he pushed himself faster and faster. The only time he turned was at the end of the hallway; he looked behind him and saw nothing but blackness before throwing open the door and hurrying out into the light. He slammed the door shut and held himself against it, but Gladhands made no attempt to open it.

The fog had dissipated and James could see the entirety of the village. The people were still surrounding the wagon, but as James approached he could see that while the ogre was still tied to the pole, Leo was standing in front of him speaking to the crowd. Their faces no longer looked the way they had; they now were just the tired and worn faces of scared villagers.

"I know you're afraid," Leo was shouting out, his little form standing resolutely in front of the ogre. "I know bad things have been happening and that this is an easy outlet. But you have to understand that this is no true ogre! He is my father, Ryan, a man you all know."

As James approached the wagon and Leo finished his speech a curious bit of magic happened. The hideous visage of the ogre began to melt away, the green turning to a normal skin color. The features shrank and transformed back into those of a man.

The ropes, originally tied to a creature three times the size of the man they now held, fell uselessly away from him.

The crowd gasped, and James almost thought that he could hear a note of disappointment in it. Having an enemy like that great hulking ogre was easy, it was an explanation for their hardships. Without it they were left with their own problems once more.

Ryan picked up his son and hugged him fiercely, tears brimming in his eyes. After a moment he put Leo down and turned to James. "Sorry about dragging you in here, but I just had to make sure that Leo was all right. I can't thank you enough for your help."

James blushed and rubbed the back of his head. He wasn't used to his cheeks burning like they were. "Yes, well. Can I get you to help me back out of the story? I think if you would boost me onto your shoulders I could get to the open page."

The fog all around the town had retreated; a warm sun shone down upon them, warming their shoulders. Without the fog he could clearly see where he had entered. There were only two paths coming from the woods, one to the page, and one to the witch's hut. They entered the path to the page.

"What did you do to the man in the suit?" Ryan asked as they walked.

James cocked one eyebrow. "I didn't do anything, actually. I

69

just ran out of there."

The smile gradually fell from Ryan's face and he looked off into the distance. "Does that mean that he will come back?"

James opened his mouth to speak, but realized that he had no words to answer the man. His tongue sat there, uncertain of how to proceed, as his stomach tightened in knots. Despite the warmth of the story, he shuddered. "I need to go home," James said.

Ryan continued scanning the horizon, his shoulders knotting up and tensing together. Though he smiled and nodded toward James, nothing about his demeanor relaxed.

They came to the spot under where the page lay open. Ryan knelt and provided a lift for James to reach back up into his father's office. Once on the other side, he turned. "I'm sure you guys will be all right. If you have more problems, you were able to come get me once, you can just do it again."

Leo smiled up at James and waved, suddenly a kid again, the entire ordeal already behind him. Ryan was not as warm, giving him a grin and a brusk wave.

As he pulled himself away from the pages, James couldn't help but feel a little of Ryan's worry himself.

*****

James went up to bed and tried to fall asleep. Amazingly, his bed had been undamaged by the ogre sitting upon it, but his stomach never stopped churning. He had done his part, hadn't he? The story was fixed, there was nothing more for him to do.

Even with the exhaustion of the adventure, when he lay down his eyes wouldn't shut. It wasn't like he was too scared to sleep, though he had certainly seen his fair share of terrifying things that day.

But he couldn't be expected to take on a thing like Gladhands, could he? How could an imaginary thing even be killed? He was just a kid, thank you very much, and he had school in the morning.

No matter how hard he worked to ignore them, little thoughts kept lifting the curtains of his eyelids as soon as they would drift down. The ticking of his clock strode mercilessly on, sounding like the crack of thunder in the silence of his room.

When the orange red of daybreak crept through his window, it fell upon James' bloodshot but wide-open eyes. With a sigh he slung his legs out of bed. It was going to be a long day, and he was going to need a good breakfast for it.

CHAPTER EIGHT

On the way to the kitchen he heard a sharp tinkling sound. It reminded him of a few months back when Mitchell threw a baseball too high and it sailed through the living room window. That was where the sound came from, too, and James walked with slow and shaking steps toward it. He peeked around the corner and saw his father sitting in their large leather chair, staring at the wall. Patrick was in his boxers and a white t-shirt with yellow stains smiling around the armpits. His hair was bed-head messed, and there were circles under his eyes. Scattered around his feet were shards of a broken glass, with droplets of scotch sprinkled around the floor like a morning dew. The smell of the alcohol soured the air.

Patrick sat and stared at nothing, the television off, no book in his hands nor notebook on his knee. He was simply sitting, and his eyes had a glazed and far away look to them.

"Dad?" James asked. His father did not respond. "Dad?" he repeated.

James shook him, and though Patrick was warm to the touch, he did not respond. A white-hot ball of panic flared up in James' stomach and he tugged harder at his father's sleeve. Patrick breathed deeply and slowly, but he did not respond to anything James did. The man's pupils were wide, unfocused. His face was slack, hanging off him like a sheet. A growth of beard stuck out of his chin.

"It's the water," a quiet voice called out from behind James.

He turned quickly, almost tripping himself up in the process. A young girl stood in the corner of the room, her hair falling in a loose braid over one shoulder, her face pinched together. She wore a simple blue blouse and a dress that hung below her knees. A pale bow was tied up in her hair and it matched the pallor of her skin.

"What do you mean?" James asked.

She took a step toward him. "It's the water. It makes them all like that. The blank stare, the loosely held muscles." She waved her hand toward Patrick. "They work and they talk and they play but when they're alone they just sit like that. You won't be able to snap him out of it." Her little shoulders slumped and she dropped her eyes to the floor. "I've tried."

"Who are you?" James asked.

"Mary. Are you the boy who's been helping us?" Her hands held together in front of her, she took a step toward him.

James nodded. He wasn't done. Of course he wasn't done. He had known that last night even as Ryan had helped him out of the page. That thing, whatever it was, Gladhands as he called himself. It would have to be taken care of. "Is there anything we can do?"

She chewed at her bottom lip. "Once it's inside you'll never really know if it's him or not. Can you help my story? I've been hiding for so long."

And just like that, James knew he would have to see this thing through to the end. A tremor went through him as he thought, just briefly, of the thing in the suit, but he swallowed hard and took her hand as she led him down the hallway back to his father's office. "What has he changed?" James asked.

The girl raised an eyebrow at him before pulling him forward more urgently. "Come, we need your help," she repeated.

The light illuminated the office again, though this time it came from an open book on the floor. There was a space on the bookshelf above that it had fallen from. The pictures on the wall of the office, of himself, of Patrick, of his mother, they all smiled down at him, and he dug his heels in and pulled Mary to a stop. "Wait."

She tugged harder at his arm, digging in with all the strength her little form could muster. James didn't move.

"I feel like I should stay with Dad until he's better. He might need me."

Mary's eyes bulged wide and she tugged again at his arm. "I'm telling you, it's the water!"

"Dad wasn't drinking water," James protested.

Finally, she dropped James' arm. Letting her chin fall to her chest, her hands balled up into tight little fists at her sides. Tears glistened down her cheeks as the little girl began to cry.

There are few things in this world more heartbreaking to hear than a crying child; it's biological, and James was certainly not immune. Thousands of years of primal instinct told him to comfort the child, to try and find what she was unhappy about and eradicate it. "Okay, okay," he gave in, "I'll try and help. Do you really think that it will help my dad if I can fix your story?"

Instantly, the little girl stopped crying and took his hand again. "Oh yes, surely it will. Come now, we need your help."

Mary stepped lightly beside the book and then leaped into it. James followed.

*****

Once more he felt himself stretch and twist as he fell down into the story. The ground came up to meet him, though this was no soft dirt he fell on. A jarring pain rang up from his knee as he slammed down onto concrete. A bruise immediately rose, purple as the blood rushed to it, and though nothing felt broken the throbbing after-effects certainly weren't pleasant.

He stood and brushed himself off, favoring one leg, the little girl nowhere to be seen. All around him stretched a city sidewalk. He was downtown somewhere, though the buildings weren't high, and there were no skyscrapers in sight. Something was slightly *off* about it all, and it took a moment for James to realize just what it was.

Putting out one hand, he jumped and then winced as he put more pressure on his hurt knee than he intended. His skin looked drained of color, there was a hint of yellow, but faded. Though James' young mind wouldn't know the word for years yet, he had seen that same sepia-toned look in old photographs.

A car drove slowly down the street, an old Buick with a pair of shark-fin lights trailing off the back. They reminded James of the old movies that his mother and father had watched a lifetime ago. A barbershop down the street had a red and white pole twirling outside the door, something James had only read about in books.

A couple walked down the sidewalk toward him. They were far enough off that he could only make out their clothes. The woman wore a simple blue sweatshirt and a long dress, the man wore a grey business suit, but as they got closer a tingle ran up James' spine and instinct kicked in. He quickly ducked into an alley behind the barbershop.

They had been smiling in an overly large, hungry way. A

feral way. A smile of predators. James waited for them to pass and then peeked his head back out at them. Their movements were similar, no, *exactly* the same. They stepped forward with each other, their shoulders bouncing up and down in perfect concordance. Their arms swung like the pendulums of a clock together. James stepped back out onto the street and began to follow them.

It was eerie, their movements. Like puppets dangling from the same string. The metaphor was so apt in James' mind that he peeked up into the sky, wondering whether a gargantuan puppet-master would be staring down at him. There was no such thing, of course. Just the faded yellow of the old portrait sky.

A diner on the corner had a wall of windows that caught his eye. He stepped up on his tip-toes, fingers pulling him up the last half an inch to the glass. There were maybe ten people in all inside, each sitting at individual tables. Their places in front of them were set the exact same: an open styrofoam box with a few pieces of lettuce, ketchup off to one side, salt and pepper to the other, and a glass of clear water right next to their left hand. A half-eaten hamburger was clutched in each of their grasps, and James cocked his head to the side as he watched them raise the burgers to their lips, bite, and chew all in accordance with one another. After they swallowed, they raised a drink of water and washed it down, smiling that ridiculous smile they all wore as they set it down.

James continued to follow the couple down the street. They never turned their heads this way or that, rather veering intently in one direction. After a few blocks the shops petered out and houses began to take over. Each house looked like a carbon copy of the other, white walls, blue roof, little gate to the back yard. It was like someone had held two mirrors to the first house and then they stretched on to infinity.

The couple seemed to be able to tell the difference between the houses, though, because they turned in the walkway of one and the man opened the front door with a key. James snuck around back, climbing over the fence and peeking in the windows. The backyards, too, all lined up in accordance. Down the row of fenced-in yards the same dog house was placed in the same area on each.

Through the window James saw the couple take off their shoes and sit in the living room, smiling all the while, and turn on the television. They never moved after that, sitting straight and tall with a few inches between them, each holding a glass of water in their hand.

There was a similarity to his father, certainly, with the blank stares, but something was different. Patrick had simply looked catatonic, hollow. These people looked mechanized; they moved and interacted, but it was all so stiff and similar.

A hand grasped James on the shoulder and another covered his mouth. Panic flared up in his stomach and he almost screamed, but then Mary's face came into view and he calmed.

"What are you doing?" she asked in a whisper.

"I don't know!" he said. "What's going on with these people? They seem like robots, or aliens. Or puppets maybe."

The little girl hazarded a peek through the window and then ducked down quickly. "It started a few weeks ago. Come with me." She led him through the back yards of the houses back toward the commercial parts of the street. They stayed low, ducking below windows as they ran. "I have an idea of where the trouble might be coming from."

They went from backyards to back alleys as they passed behind the row of shops. They had to stop once as a shopkeeper, smiling, stepped into the back and dropped a bag of trash in a bin.

Once beyond the commercial part of the town they came to a series of larger, boxy buildings. Ducking through the buildings they came to a large beige factory, with twin smokestacks rising up into the air puffing out great grey clouds of smoke. Mary pulled him along, the urgency of her movement increasing the closer they got. A metal staircase wound up the side of the building to a door, and though their footsteps rang out loudly along the steps, they moved quickly. Once inside the building James saw what a nightmare truly looked like.

They stood on a metal boardwalk, fifty feet above the main floor. Below them large cylinders of liquid stood to one side, though that wasn't what caused James' eyes to open wide with fear. Scuttling around holding long wooden paddles in the liquid were some of the biggest spiders James had ever seen. They were stirring it, tending to it with their grotesquely hairy legs. There were hundreds of them milling around, tending to the cylinders, but even that wasn't the worst. Where the cylinders ended the true horror began. Splayed out on a red carpet was the largest and hairiest spider of them all, five times the size of the others, its abdomen swollen and shining with a greasy sheen. It was laid on its back, propped against the side of the wall, squirting a clumpy stream of eggs out onto the floor. These were then picked up by smaller spiders with one set of their eight legs and carried over to the cylinders where they were mixed in with the liquid. Finally, this liquid was being drained into bottles and labeled as 'purified water.'

"We have to stop it," Mary said. "Then we can get my parents back." She quietly ran off across the walkway. James started to follow.

A hand descended on his shoulder, a thin and skeletal hand

that stopped him in his tracks. "You can't change this one," a voice said.

His blood froze in his veins, causing him to tingle all over. His hair stood straight on the back of his neck. He had never felt more exposed, more vulnerable. James turned, slowly, and looked up at the smiling face of Gladhands. "Why not?" he said lamely, his mouth dry, feeling like it was filled with cotton.

The masked thing knelt down beside him, exuding a smell like worms and dirt, and smiled. "My child, I haven't done anything to this story. This is how your father wrote it."

CHAPTER NINE

Fear is a funny thing. In some cases, it can assist you, allowing young mothers the strength to lift entire cars off of their children. The burst of adrenaline that accompanies fear can make you run faster than you've ever run in your life, be stronger than you ever thought possible. Some times, however, it can take away reason completely and leave you a quivering mess.

*****

The fear that James felt in that instant, looking up at the grinning visage of Gladhands, took away any movement possible from his legs. His tongue felt thick, and the only thing he could think to do was argue. "You're lying," he said, "my father writes fairy tales. Fairy tales always have a happy ending."

Gladhands let out a great laugh and held his gloved hands over his stomach. "My child, you have much to learn both about fairy tales and your father's writing. You see Mary there?" he asked, pointing down to where the small girl was sneaking. "She does all this in the story. The spiders lay their eggs in the water supply and the people drink it, hatching little spiderlings in their brains. The entire town is taken over except Mary, who tries to kill the queen spider. Can you guess what happens then? She gets captured until her parents come, at which point the queen spider feeds little Mary to them. It happens over and over again."

"That's awful!" James said.

"Isn't it though?" Gladhands said gleefully, rubbing his hands together. "It's one of my favorites. But you can see why Mary wanted you to change it, right? She doesn't want to live in this story. She's like all the others, she just wants to have a happy story where nothing much happens and everyone always gets along. But that's not a worthwhile story, that's not a story at all. That's just stagnation."

"Is that why you changed the others?" James asked.

"One of the reasons. Though the main reason is that this is how your father *used* to write. His tales were wonderful then, you would fall in love with a character and just watch their world get torn apart right on the page in front of you." Gladhands licked at his lips. "The misery, the sorrow, the abject despair! The fear! The hopelessness! It all tasted so delicious." He shivered at the memory, a large smile plastered on his bolted-on face. It was like a living thing, his mask, it had all the movement of a face but was clearly affixed to his skull. The mask fell into a scowl and Gladhands pointed a finger at James.

"But then that whore mother of yours came along. He couldn't feel bad when she was around, and he lost his appetite for sorrow, for despair. Happy endings were *everywhere.*" Gladhands turned and spat in disgust. "I had less and less to eat, and so I grew smaller and smaller in your father. And when you came along I thought I was all but finished. Oh sure, I'd get my time in around the holidays or if you and your mother were gone, but eating only a few times a year starves a beast."

Gladhands leaned over the railing, his gloved hand on his chin. "But then a miracle happened. The accident. I probably would have been permanently crippled had it not been for the accident."

Something jarred loose in James and he began to back away from Gladhands. He couldn't keep listening to that...*thing* talk about his mother and father.

"The first few days were a numb grief, something I could work with, sure, but not ideal. But as the days went by there was more to eat and I grew stronger. My voice was heard again, my soft little whispers in the night. Guilt was my way back. Guilt and sorrow."

Gladhands whirled suddenly and grabbed James' shirt neck. "You smell of fear. You're leaking it right now." He sniffed James and licked the side of his face slowly with his cold, wet tongue that smelled of rotting fish. He moaned with pleasure, smacking his lips with a relish. "I can taste it on you. You're thinking of running, of getting back to your little hole to your other world, aren't you?" He smiled and laughed that high-pitched laugh again. It sent a tremor through James. "But you can't go. I closed the book, and I think I'll keep it hidden away from you. My voice grows louder with every passing thought, every niggling and nagging doubt inside your father. I've wormed my way in, and I'm growing stronger."

James kicked out suddenly, catching the beast in the stomach. Seeing his opportunity, he sprinted away from the monster. Gladhands' laughter echoed all around him, his voice piercing through the air.

James made the mistake of looking back just as he thought for a moment he was free. Gladhands was climbing the ceiling of the factory, his neck twisted around, his mouth open and dripping saliva. The monster scuttled over James and fell to the boardwalk, blocking his way.

"There really is no hope for you," Gladhands said. "You're trapped here, trapped and alone. You might as well let me eat you now."

"He's not alone!" a voice cried out from behind James. He turned and saw Jewel, the beautiful dark-haired woman he had saved from being eaten by the witch. She opened her mouth wide and began to sing, the sound beautiful and piercing, filling James' heart with hope.

It was like a breath of air to a drowning man. Warmth spread through James' legs and he felt strong, capable, loved even.

Gladhands covered his ears and hissed at the two of them, falling to his knees and clutching at his head as Jewel and James backed away on the boardwalk.

"You think you can hide from me in your father's stories?" Gladhands cried out as they opened the door. "You haven't even seen how dark they get, you won't survive them. I'll find you! That bitch can't stay with you forever!"

Jewel slammed the door to the factory and they ran down the steps and away from the beige building. Ahead of them, down the street toward where James had originally entered the page, people began to walk out of their houses *en masse*. Smiling blank-eyed faces streamed toward them, arms and legs marching in unison.

Jewel pulled him along, her long legs able to move much faster than his short stubby ones. They ducked into the barbershop once they reached the red and white spinning pole. "Wait, we'll be trapped," James said.

"No, there's a tunnel here to another story. We may not be able to get you back just yet, but we can sure get you out of here. It's not the most pleasant of stories, be forewarned, but no one will be actively chasing after us there. Let's go!" She pulled him through the barbershop main lobby and then the back room lined with chairs and mirrors and clippings of hair in the trash bins. Stopping at the woman's restroom, she pushed James inside.

"Wait, this is for ladies!" he said.

She cocked an eye at him, a look of complete exasperation on her face. "It's not a restroom, no one actually uses the bathroom in a story. Just go, I'll head them off and try to meet you later." With a grunt she pushed him as hard as she could into the darkness of the women's restroom.

*****

He fell backward, though rather than falling onto tile or porcelain as he expected he fell into a pile of snow. The door closed in front of him as snow trickled down the back of his neck, causing him to shiver involuntarily. He sat up and shook his head. The door to the women's restroom was still in front of him, though that was all that existed of that other world. It stood thin and tall like a monolith, the black and brass colored plaque reading 'Ladies' in curlicue writing, but the world around it was different. There was no barbershop nor mobs of smiling, spider-infested suburbanites around; the city he had been in just moments before had vanished. All but the solitary door.

He was in a large snow-covered field. Little bits of cornstalks stuck up out of the white. At the edge of the field barren trees formed a barrier. About fifty feet from where he lay a mound of snow jutted up higher than the rest of the field. James walked to it; he wasn't sure that Jewel would be able to lead those...*things* away from the entrance to this story and he wanted to be far away if they were going to be coming through. His breath came out in a fog as he trundled across the field.

The protrusion turned out to be a glass window. There was a room underneath it. The sunlight fell through and illuminated a tiled floor, white and black, like a checkerboard. A set of stairs wound around the glass, a brass knob at the top. James pulled the handle and was delighted to find that the glass opened freely, allowing him to enter the warmth of the stairway.

At the bottom he found himself in a sort of underground tunnel stretching out on either side of him. It looked like something a train or subway would ride through, but there were no tracks on the ground, just tile. The walls were bare and echoed the sound of a hushed conversation down to him. He walked toward the voices, stepping gently so as not to make a sound.

The hallway twisted down and back around on itself. As the conversation grew louder, James was able to pick out bits and pieces of one side of it.

"Your heart feels a little heavy," a quiet and speculative voice said. "Let's see. Hmm. A little less than a pound. That is heavy. Average is between a half and three-quarters of a pound. At least in those that I've come across."

At the end of the hallway a bright blue light shone through a domed entrance. James crept up to the room, holding his breath, tiptoeing gently. After the last story he felt he should be more wary and not assume every tale was a happy one.

"Tongue is thick. My my, must be quite the linguist. A little under three pounds, heavy, heavy."

Steeling himself, James peeked through the entrance. There was one man laid back in a reclined chair, his back to the entrance, with another leaning over him, looking intently at something in his hand. He wore a pair of magnifying lenses attached to his glasses and had a scholarly look of interest in a lumpy red thing he held. After a moment he placed it in a bin beside him.

"How well do you say you keep things in perspective?" the man with scholarly interest asked before turning to a table mounted to the seat. "Could you keep perspective if you could only see two dimensions?" He picked up a small metal instrument shaped like a miniature ice cream scoop. "Perspective is a very important thing to keep."

A small detail, something he had missed before, stood out to him. There were thick leather straps around the man in the chair. The body was shaking slightly, struggling, but the bands were so tight that it could only move an inch or so in either direction.

Scholarly Interest leaned forward with the ice cream scoop. A shrill scream echoed down the hallway as Scholarly Interest's forearms flexed and he dug into the front of the man's face. Finally he pulled out a white, egg-looking thing with a thin strand of red mucus attached to it. James put a hand up to his mouth to keep himself from gagging when he realized what it was.

Scholarly Interest took off his magnifying glasses and held the severed eye up to his own. "Ah, you don't seem able to keep a good perspective at all. It's quite grey, looking through your eyes, did you know that? I would assume that everyone thinks they see the world in a *normal* way," he put up two bloody air quotes as he said this, "I sometimes get a rosy vision when I look through others' eyes. Not yours. I'll be right back, I'm going to pop this on the projector while it's still fresh." Scholarly Interest stood and walked through a door on the other side of the room as James ducked back into the hallway.

When the coast was clear he edged his way into the room itself. It was designed disturbingly like a dentist's office, the reclining chair, the pictures of bland people smiling on the walls, the tray of gleaming instruments. James approached the reclining man with small steps, tiptoeing his way across the tile. When he was able to get around to the front, he gasped.

There was no doubt about who it was in the chair. James had seen pictures of him when he was this young, no more than twenty years old, but even if he hadn't he would know that face anywhere. He was looking down at his father on the table, though young Patrick was missing a substantial amount of himself. His eye socket was empty and there was a gaping space where his heart should be. Some of his organs lay in a bowl next to him.

James had to remind himself that this was a story, a story that his father had written himself. This wasn't real, it was just words on a page. But why would his father write something so dark? Was this one of the earlier stories that Gladhands had hinted about? Was this the way he always used to write?

The sound of footsteps told him that Scholarly Interest was coming back. He ran to the other side of the hallway, to where the tunnel lead.

"I think I can fix you," Scholarly Interest said, "but we're going to have to resort to some pretty extreme measures. I'm going to have to take a look at that brain of yours."

The sudden high-pitched sound of a saw whined in the other room. These certainly weren't the stories that his father had let him read at all. The stories that his father wrote for him were fairy tales with happy endings, moral fables about how to lead a good life. This, this was something else completely. The words of Gladhands came back to him, *you haven't even seen how dark they get!*

It was true. He felt very small and very alone here in this story as the sound of the buzz saw whined in the background. Was this truly his father? It couldn't be, it had to be Gladhands taking over, the man he knew could never dream up something that awful. How long had that monster been lurking inside of his dad?

A hand clasped over his mouth and he felt himself pulled backwards into the darkness of the tunnel. Jewel held him, a finger up to her lips, and when he recognized her she let him go.

"We have to go this way, there's another story down a little ways," she said.

"Hmm," the voice of Scholarly Interest floated down to them. "I think I see the issue. Do you have a spider problem at home? Your brain looks like it might have been healthy once, but a spider got in here and laid a bunch of eggs. Looks like they've been eating for a while now."

James shuddered. "It's not like this one, is it?" He whispered to Jewel, "I don't know how much more of stories like this I can take."

"You have to understand," Jewel said, taking his hand. She lead him away from the operating room. "There's a balance to all these. I've been traveling between them all my life, but there are some that I don't even dare enter." There were no lights in the tunnel, but James could feel the air gradually warming. With a sense of complete trust he held her hand firmly, willing to go wherever she lead him. "It's always been a struggle, but we were able to keep the balance in check pretty well up until a few years ago. I think something happened to the creator, and now Gladhands is getting stronger."

As they were running through the darkness of the tunnel a light began to shine at the end of it. James was finally able to see the ground he was running over. They reached the end and the tunnel opened up into a field of green grass and trees with leaves and flowers blossoming from them. The sun shone brightly overhead, warming James' blood in an instant.

"Where are we?" James asked.

Jewel smiled, and the warmth of her face matched that of the sun overhead. As he looked up at her James felt something grow in him, a heady, giddy nervous energy. He felt comfortable and safe in that instant, looking up at Jewel. She squeezed his hand. "We're in one of my favorite stories, come quickly."

CHAPTER TEN

He had so many questions as they walked. The little tunnel behind them seemed no more than a hole in the ground, and the memory of Scholarly Interest faded fast. Grass was all around, he had never been in such a large field. There were no houses spotting the landscape, just nature. He felt his lungs open wide in the fresh air, the smell of spring delighting his senses.

"Is this a good story? What happens in it?" James asked.

She squeezed his hand in response. "Patience child. Experience the thing, you don't need to know everything before it happens."

For a moment James wondered at the fact that he was still holding hands with Jewel. It wasn't like he had known her long, but it felt natural. He shrugged the thought away.

They traveled over a field of green and through a small patch of trees, stopping on the crest of a hill. James gasped in awe as he took in the sight below him. They were on the side of a great valley. To one side a castle made of stone stood tall, colorful streamers flying from each corner, a great wooden door pulled up over a water-filled moat. On the other side of the valley a volcano dwarfed everything, the clouds red and swirling around its peak.

Though it was one of the most breathtaking sights he had ever seen, some little niggling thought tugged at him. Somehow he *knew* this place. Not seen, though, he had never seen the place before. Imagined.

"Come, the feast shall begin soon," Jewel said, pulling him along toward the castle. She took him away from the main gate, toward the side where a tree had fallen over the moat, creating a makeshift bridge. The log itself was not more than two feet wide, they had to cross single file, but they made it and were able to enter the servants' door.

The sound of a festival broke over them the second the door opened. Inside was a cavernous hall with long tables laid out through the middle. Men and women in leather armor sat at the tables, raucously eating roasted bits of meat. The smell of food was overwhelmingly tantalizing; James' mouth began to salivate the instant they stepped inside. The noise of joyous feasting echoed off the high stone walls, overwhelming his senses.

Jewel caught the eye of a giant of a man and he waved a turkey drumstick at her. He was clearly in the middle of illustrating a story to the people around him, his arms flailing around wildly. They approached the table and squeezed in, catching the last of the tale.

"So he comes at me, and I parry his thrust, of course," he said, using the drumstick as a sword, "and I swing mightily on the rebound, catching him right above the shoulder. Well he stumbles back and the dumb bastard's legs trip over his own helmet. He was down on the ground and I stood over him, my blade at his throat, and I simply told him, 'Never steal from my plate again, my food is my food.'"

"Truly," Jewel said, "it sounds like a terrifying foe that you vanquished."

"To what do we owe the honor, Jewel? 'Tis not every day us lowly warriors have the pleasure of such fine company."

Jewel reached forward and picked a bit of turkey out of the large man's beard, smiling as she did. "Adlan, do you know where I can find Iqbhaal? I have something important to talk with him about."

The man waved a grease-stained hand toward the other end of the hall. "Doubtless he's in study. High-nosed bastard never comes to feast with us, always has a servant bring him his food. Do me a favor, when you see the wizard give him a good swift kick in the pants for me, see if you can't dislodge whatever is stuck up there."

Jewel stifled a giggle. "Will do, Adlan." She lead James over to a stone staircase on the other side of the hallway. As they walked more than a few people turned their heads, though it wasn't Jewel that they were looking at. James blushed and wiped at his face, checking his shirt for stains. Was he that out of place there?

"What story is this?" James asked.

"It's called 'Jamie and the Dragon,' and it's one of my absolute favorites. I spend most of my time here when I'm not in my own story."

"Jamie?" he asked, the hairs rising on the back of his head. "My dad used to call me that when I was little."

She turned, and for a moment a sly smile appeared on her face. "I know," she said.

James continued to follow her up the stairs, his eyebrows furrowed. A vague memory from long ago surfaced in his mind. He had heard that story before. Long ago his father used to read to him every night before he went to bed, his father and mother both, actually, though his mother usually just sat and listened. She was there, though, now that he thought more about it.

"Jewel?" James asked suddenly.

She stopped on the staircase and turned. "Yes?"

"How is it that you know so much about all these other stories? Do all the other characters know this much?"

Her smile faltered for a moment, like the flickering of a candle in the wind. "Your father sometimes reuses characters. It

98

gives them a few extra dimensions. I've been around for a while, and I like to travel through the other stories."

"Why? Why travel through the other stories?" he asked.

She chewed at her lip, a small gesture. After a moment she spoke, though it was in a solemn whisper, as though she were on sacred ground. "Maybe I feel like it's the best way to stay in contact with the creator."

James was about to ask her to clarify when she hushed him. They were at the top of the steps, standing outside a wooden door. She pushed it open quietly.

Behind the door there was a library, with candles burning in sconces on the wall and a fire roaring in the fireplace, even though the temperature was mild enough. A stooped old man sat in a leather chair poring over a thickly bound book. He had glasses perched on the end of his curved nose and he was muttering to himself, the tip of his beard quivering above the page he was on.

"Iqbhaal?" Jewel said.

He looked up from his book with a snarl, his eyebrows crunched together. When he saw them, though, his face relaxed and his eyes opened wide, his mouth dropping into a smile. "Jewel, hello. Who do you," he began, only to stop and adjust his glasses. "Oh my, is that who I think it is?" he asked.

She nodded and then brought James forward into the light.

The old man studied him intently, making him feel like a bug under a microscope.

"The son of the creator?" Iqbhaal asked. Jewel nodded again. The old man stood immediately, the book falling off his lap to lie on the ground. Iqbhaal paid no attention to it. He strode forward and seized James' hand, thrusting it up and down vigorously. "My word, I cannot think to thank you enough for coming."

"My name's James," he said, unsure of this strange old man.

"And I am Iqbhaal, at your service," the man said, bowing low.

He had never been bowed to before, and he wasn't quite sure that he liked it, so he strode around the room, fingering the dusty books upon the shelf. The room bore a remarkable similarity to his father's office, though with the addition of the fireplace. "Do you know how I can get home?" he asked. "I need to get back to my dad, I don't think he's doing okay."

Though James thought it was an innocent enough question, Iqbhaal reacted in a remarkably troubled way. His mouth dropped open and he had to put a hand out to his desk to steady himself. "The creator is sick?" He strode to the fireplace and put a hand to his chin, stroking the thick beard that clung there. "Of course, that would make sense. The enemy has been growing stronger steadily. He is making headway into our stories, I have even heard reports that he is changing some of them, occupying them for himself."

"I can tell you for a fact that this is true," Jewel said. "It happened to mine. He silenced my song, and in doing so kept me trapped by the witch, damned to repeat the worst of it over and over again."

Iqbhaal turned, his mouth still open in shock. "But, my dear, how did you get out?"

Jewel turned and placed a hand on James' shoulder. "It was only through the actions of the son. I brought him through and he was able to free me, but Gladhands is growing stronger."

Iqbhaal held his hands up to his ears and shook his head. "Say not his name, you'll bring him here."

"Iqbhaal, something needs to be done. I understand his necessity, but there has to be a balance. He has become too powerful. If we don't do something about him soon, he'll take over all of the stories. We don't even know how far he's gotten."

"So do you know how I can get back?" James repeated. He had been ignored before, children often are when they have something to say, but this was especially important. This was about his dad. He couldn't stop thinking about him, about the catatonic state James had left him in.

The old man walked to the open window and stood with his hands behind his back. "He can never get here, that much we know. I say we wait, there is nothing else that we can do and to strike out would be to risk too many of us."

Jewel curled her hands into tight little fists. "That can't possibly be your advice," she said. "Do you really think that Gladhands of all people is just going to decide that he's done? That he's had enough?"

Iqbhaal turned with a quickness that made James take a step back. "What would you have me do? Gladhands can change a story. Do you understand that? Do you understand how dangerous that is?" The old man shuddered violently. "If you only knew some of the things I've heard."

Jewel pulled James in front of her and placed her hands lightly on his shoulders. "James can too. When my story got changed he was the one to change it back. Send him through the stories. He can find out why Gladhands is growing so strong. Maybe once we know then we will have some way of reversing all of this."

James finally had enough, the world always ignored children, and he was sick of them speaking like he wasn't even in the room, like he wasn't important enough to treat like an equal. "Hey! I'm right here, why don't you answer my question?" he shouted and the torches in the room flickered, a tremor passing through the building. The floor shook, a few books fell off the bookshelf, and James held out his arms to steady himself. After a moment everything calmed and the two adults were looking at him wide-eyed and astonished.

Iqbhaal was the first to react. He knelt down and placed a hand on James' shoulder. "I'm sorry, you're right. I shouldn't have ignored your question. It's easy to get back to your world. All you have to do is go back through the same page that you came through and you can leave us to deal with the problems here."

A sinking feeling began in the pit of James' stomach, a sourness that pulled low. "The exact same?" he asked. "Can't I find a different one?"

Iqbhaal shook his head slowly. "No, it has to be the exact page that brought you here. Do you remember the story you came through? The page should still be there."

James swallowed hard. "Gladhands told me that he took it. I didn't think it would be a problem, I was so concerned with just getting away from him."

The old man stood, his knee cracking, and he let out a big sigh. "You're trapped here then. We'll find you a story you like and get you set up in there. I'm sure you'll be able to make a life that you will be satisfied with. At least until Gladhands stops this mad advancement into the other stories."

"You can't be serious," Jewel said with a sneer. "Just give up and live here? That's the advice that you give him? Who are you, Iqbhaal? I don't know this coward in front of me."

Iqbhaal picked up the book he had been reading and threw it across the room. "What would you have me do? Condemn a child, the son of the creator no less, to a fool's mission? Do you really think that a child can overcome the enemy when even you can't?"

She walked to the old man and placed a hand on his shoulder, speaking to him quietly. "I'm sorry, Iqbhaal. I shouldn't have spoken to you like that. It's not our decision anyway. I think we should leave it to James, it is his life, and he has to do what he thinks is best." She turned to James and sat down on the floor so she could look at him on an even level. "It's your call. We can certainly find you a story that you feel comfortable in and help you set up a life there if that's what you want."

"I need to get back. My dad needs me. What's the alternative?" James asked, his voice sounding much smaller than he would have liked.

"The alternative is trying to sneak through the stories to get to Gladhands. He's like me, he tends to wander, but he also has one that's just his. We can try and steal the page back, getting you back home so you can help your dad get better."

James furrowed his brow. He didn't quite understand the rules of this place. It was easy when he could go into one story and then out, but this was all getting very complicated. He felt very small and very alone. "Can't we just skip straight to that story?"

Her lips pursed, Jewel shook her head. "Could you just skip to the other side of your world? You're going to have to make your way through many stories before you get to his. It won't be easy, but I can try and help where I can. But like I said, it's all your choice."

Choice? It didn't feel like a choice to James. The one thing he knew for sure was that he had to get home. "All right, I'll go and try to recover the page, but I don't exactly know where I'm going."

Iqbhaal tapped at his chin, his brow furrowed. "You'll need some protection. Even before the stories began to change, there were some tales of the creator that I wouldn't have advised wandering through. There's the armor of Tantuk here in this story, if you can get to it, and then you would still need a sword."

"I don't even know how to hold a sword," James said.

"That doesn't mean you shouldn't have one."

Jewel had a strange look on her face, one of wonderment and curiosity. "Iqbhaal, what about the Arbiter?"

The old man burst out laughing. "You really like to shoot for the stars, don't you, Jewel?"

"What's the Arbiter?" James asked.

"Why is that so strange? It was written for a 'Jamie' story anyway," Jewel said.

Iqbhaal knelt again by James. "The Arbiter is a sword in one of the other stories."

"Wouldn't one sword be just as good as another?" James asked.

"No," Jewel replied. "The Arbiter is a sword unlike any other. It senses the intentions of a person, it weighs their heart and responds to that. Now, theoretically, if a person were to be completely neutral for the entirety of their life, the sword would be just a sword. But against someone that is evil, it would inflict exponential damage, and lend strength to any that were good."

"The problem," Iqbhaal interrupted, "is that it is made for only one person. Little Jamie. He uses it to defeat a demon knight."

Jewel stood, a look of determination on her face. "I think James will be able to wield it."

James looked between the two. "So where do I find the sword?"

"First things first," Iqbhaal said. "You'll need the armor of Tantuk."

"Didn't you say it was right in this story?" James asked.

"Well, let's get it."

"It is in this story," Iqbhaal admitted, "but," he hesitated, "it won't be the easiest to get."

"Why? Where is it? Why won't it be easy to get?"

Jewel and Iqbhaal looked at the same time out of the window, across the field, to where the volcano sat quietly churning. "Because a dragon is guarding it."

CHAPTER ELEVEN

Jewel and James stood to one side as Iqbhaal packed up some things in a pouch. The man wore a robe with seemingly a thousand pockets; he picked up things off his desk and they just disappeared on his person. "Why do we need this armor, can't James use any other from the weapons depot?" Jewel asked.

Iqbhaal started to answer and then looked down at James. Now, despite popular opinion, children are not stupid. They are a lot more observant than we often give them credit for. James knew the look, almost as if he could read Iqbhaal's mind. There was something that he wanted to tell Jewel that he didn't want James to hear. James, with a sigh, went over to the other end of the office and studied the books on the shelf intently.

He caught snatches of the conversation but most of it was lost as they whispered to one another. "...heard rumors about how he...cavum worms...protects the heart, doesn't allow...can't have the *son* of the creator...could destroy the entire..."

Finally, they turned to him, their secret conversation over with. "I think Iqbhaal is right," Jewel said. Her face was drained of all of its color and her lips were pursed tightly in the corners. "The armor of Tantuk is necessary."

James curled his lip at them. "Is it? Well I'm glad you made that decision for me. Great, so a dragon is guarding what we need. What happens now?"

"We go there," Jewel said, pointing up the side of the volcano.

*****

As the three made their way out the side of the servants' door a voice called out to them. "Wait!" it cried, the sound almost lost in a raucous clanging of armor. Around the corner came Adlan, the huge warrior from the feast. They stopped and turned, and when he got to them he bent over double, trying to catch his breath. "Where are you going?" he asked when he could finally get the words out.

"Up there," James said, pointing to the volcano.

Adlan's eyes grew large. "You're going to the dragon?" He balled up his fists and smiled hugely at them before jumping up and down. "I knew it! Can I come?"

It was such a surreal moment; Adlan, this great hulking man, looked as excited as a child about the prospect of going to a dragon's den.

"Why would you want to?" Jewel asked. "You don't even get all the way there in this story."

"That's just it!" Adlan said, gripping the handle of a large broadsword on his belt. As he did so James noticed the massive amount of weapons that the man carried. There were knives and axes, even a flail, all strapped at different points on his body. "I've never been there. This entire story everyone is afraid of the thing, and then getting hyped up to go fight it, and then right as everyone is charging up the mountain a pack of goblins comes up from behind us and *I* have to stay back and defend against them. It's not fair."

Jewel and James locked eyes. "It really couldn't hurt, could it?" James asked.

Iqbhaal gave the sweating behemoth a disapproving look. "I suppose, in case we need someone to do grunt work," he said before turning and walking up toward the volcano.

Adlan flicked his chin in an obscene gesture towards the wizard's back and James giggled. The big man gave him an exaggerated wink before setting off.

James and Jewel walked side by side. "Jewel?" he asked. "Who *is* Gladhands?"

Her face fell and she took a deep breath. "I can't really answer that for you. I can tell you that he was around a long time before even I was created. He has his own story, but I've never dared venture close to it, and he seems to pop up a lot in others."

The image of the monster's hungry eyes as he talked of fear and despair made James shiver and put the thought away. As he did so another, unbidden, thought came bubbling to the surface. It was of his father's face right before he went into the story, blank and lifeless, the way he hadn't responded to being shaken, even though his skin was warm. Gladhands had done something to his father, that much was certain. He took a deep breath and felt a sense of determination fill him.

They reached the base of the volcano quicker than he would have assumed, though it now loomed over them. "There's a path that we can follow," Iqbhaal said. "Follow me."

"So who is this Tantuk guy and why do I need his armor?" James asked. Iqbhaal and Jewel looked sharply at him and then turned away.

"His armor gets used by little Jamie against the dragon." Adlan said. "Oh bugger off, you two. You look at me like I'm poisoning him or something. The kid's got a right to know, doesn't he? The dragon in this story instills fear, not hatred or anger, simple fear. He exudes it, trying to worm his way into your heart. The armor of Tantuk was the armor of a warrior immune to fear, though it only covers the left side of your chest, so it's worthless in other regards. But in this story specifically, it allows Jamie to defeat the dragon."

"So why do I need his armor? It seems like something else,

something that covered my entire chest, might be better for me."

Iqbhaal hushed the two of them. "We are almost at the entrance to the cave. Now is not the time for questions!"

They were, too, though to James it felt like they had barely traveled twenty feet. Looking back he saw the castle far below them, no larger in his vision than a child's toy.

There seemed to be a path etched around the volcano that led into the side, much too small for a dragon to enter but just large enough for them to squeeze through. Purposefully they lit no torches, feeling their way through the dark with Iqbhaal leading them. When they got to the end and saw the lumbering lizard snoring in his cave, James felt a concoction of emotions he had never quite experienced before.

*****

Now, when most people imagine themselves meeting a dragon for the first time, the only thing they think about is the fear that they would have. And really, that's a logical thing. Dragons are gigantic creatures thousands of years old, with teeth as large as your arm. They could swallow you whole as easily as you could swallow an aspirin. But what most people who have actually seen a dragon tell you about is the fierce sense of awe and wonderment they felt. James felt that jaw-dropping amazement and almost ran up to touch the thing when he first saw it, a move that would have been extremely unwise.

*****

Luckily for them, Erebus, as this particular dragon was known, was fast asleep; otherwise James' initial step into the room might have been his last. The creature was massive, curled up in a room full of trinkets and treasures. Its snores rumbled through the cavern in the volcano. The claws on the tips of its fingers were long as swords, and looked twice as sharp.

The ground he lay upon was littered with gold and jewels, and Iqbhaal looked this way and that trying to find the armor. "It's here somewhere, usually it's little Jamie that finds it, I've never had to look for it myself."

A glimmer of shining red caught James' attention. A small shoulder plate, tinted blood red, sat on a pile of gold just behind the dragon. Without thinking twice, he set off tiptoeing toward it.

When James got closer to the dragon he felt the fear. It oozed off the creature in hot waves, causing his stomach to feel like it was filled with curdled milk. His breathing came quicker and blood pounded in his ears, but he forced himself forward.

As soon as he touched the armor he felt the fear disappear, though not completely. He still felt it, but it was muted, like hearing someone through a pane of glass. The armor itself was simple, just a piece of red leather and metal that fit around his left shoulder and draped down to cover his heart, but he felt himself affected by it. His courage bolstered, he made his way back to the rest of the party. The dragon slumbered on. Jewel helped him strap the armor across him; he rather liked the look it gave him. He felt like a knight, like he could slay that dragon single-handedly should it wake. Jewel must have seen a look in his eye, because she pulled him back into the tunnel before he could do anything remotely like that.

As everyone else moved back in the tunnel, Adlan stepped out, a small smile on his face. He took a moment, just looking around at everything, before nodding and turning his back.

"You don't really expect to steal from a dragon and get away with it, do you?" Adlan asked as they made their way back down the volcano. "He'll find it missing soon enough."

Iqbhaal nodded. "It is an unfortunate necessity. Things will be strange here for a while, but I will try to keep them under control."

"Why?" James asked. "Why is it necessary? Why can't I just have regular armor?"

His question was cut off, however, by an ear-splitting roar that shook the side of the volcano. They all looked up, and high above them a gigantic shadow blotted out the sun. The dragon rose up, its wings so great that it threw much of the valley into shadow, and flew straight toward the castle.

"Oh dear," Iqbhaal said. "We have to get back quickly. The fighting will start soon."

They rushed down the side of the volcano and across the prairie. The dragon was on the other side of the castle, tearing at the walls with his teeth and claws and billowing out black smoke. The group rushed in the servants' door, the same that they had come out of, and hurried through the castle. The festive shouts had been replaced with harried ones, and the tinkle of silverware with the clink of armor as everyone gathered at the battlements to prepare for the dragon.

"We'll have to separate," Iqbhaal said, stopping at the top of a staircase. "I am needed here to help fight this beast. Hurry back with the armor when you have done what you need to do."

He ran off away from them toward where people were shouting and gathering weapons. Adlan stayed back.

"Aren't you going to go help with the dragon?" James asked.

"I been thinking about that," Adlan said. "I got to see it, that's really good enough for me. I was thinking that maybe I could come with you guys, I bet I could be a lot of help."

James eyed him warily. The hulking man slumped his shoulders, as though he were trying to make himself smaller, and gave an awkward little smile. The weapons all around him jingled and banged together; he was a walking cacophony of clatters and clanks. "I don't know, we may have to be stealthy, and no offense, but it doesn't really look like stealth is your strong point."

Adlan nodded quickly. "Right you are, little man, right you are. But you don't know the ways of the stories like I do. I'm like Jewel, I do my fair share of traveling, and I might know places even she doesn't."

"James said no," Jewel interrupted, "and that should be enough of an answer for you."

"What are you going to do if you guys find yourselves in the pits of the wendigo, or the hills of the fenris? Child, do you know what the wendigo are?"

James shook his head.

"The wendigo look like corpses, but they're not dead."

"Like zombies?" James asked. He had seen those in movies before, they didn't frighten him. They moved far too slowly to ever catch a quick child like himself. Sometimes, late at night, he thought that it might even be kind of *fun* to have the world break out in zombies. School would get canceled, and that jerk

Kenny Halvorford would surely be one of the first eaten.

Adlan shook his head slowly. "No, not like zombies. I'd take a graveyard full of zombies any day over the wendigo. You see, the wendigo look like skeletons with skin still on 'em, and they're fairly fast moving. Once they catch you they give you the kiss, try and imagine that, something barely above a corpse, smelling like death, locking lips with you and just sucking your humanity out of you. Then they take your form, see, so they can sneak up on those you love without them being suspicious, but they have to do it quickly, because their flesh dies fast. They only have a few hours before they're back looking like the walking dead. They're the only thing I'm truly afraid of, but there's so much evil that's come out of the creator, you have to wonder what's gone wrong inside him."

Jewel slapped Adlan across the face and he stood quickly. "What was that for?"

"That's James' father you're talking about, as well as your own creator. Show a little respect."

"Who says I have to?" Adlan said with complete indignation. "I didn't ask to be written. Look, my point was just that there's a lot out there, and you're just a boy and a girl with a song. You might need someone who can stick a sword in something."

James felt a chill run down the back of his spine. The thought of dead rotting lips sucking his essence out of him and then wearing him like a coat terrified him. He pictured the wendigo form of himself, shambling around, desperately hungry for a new victim. "Adlan, you can come. It can't hurt and you may be able to help us."

"Are you sure?" Jewel asked. "I'm sure we can do just fine without this great big pile of worthless."

James nodded and Adlan smiled. "You won't regret it for a minute. I've been so tired of this story, it'll be good to get a little more adventure, be a central character for once. I'm sick of that little turd Jamie getting all the spotlight." James laughed and tried to stifle it with his hand. Adlan raised his eyebrows and looked to Jewel. "What's so funny?"

"I'm that little turd," James said, finally releasing the laughter. "My dad made that story for me."

Adlan cleared his throat and turned a bright shade of red. "Well, I'm glad to see you've grown up a bit. No offense meant of course."

James waved the comment away and started back down the hallway with Jewel and Adlan following after him. The entrance to the next story was in the lower portions of the castle, past even the dungeon. Jewel led them on through the winding hallways, further and further down, as the sounds of battle slowly receded above them.

"Stop here," Jewel said. A turn in the hallway had led them

to a large thing covered in a purple sheet. She tugged at the edge of the sheet, unveiling the thing underneath.

It was an oval mirror trimmed with gold. It looked like any old vanity mirror, maybe a bit larger than most, but the glass itself had a shimmering, liquid quality to it. A thin layer of dust lay across the golden vines that wound themselves around the trim. Jewel motioned James toward it.

A thought bubbled up in James. "How exactly do we know where we're going? It's not as though we're following a map or anything."

"The stories all fit together like pages in a book, though you won't experience it that way," Jewel said. "You may experience it differently from story to story. From one it may be a crossing of a mountain, in another it is as simple as opening a door. Does that make sense?"

James scrunched up his face, trying to picture it in his mind. She had spoken to him like an adult, and he wanted it to stay that way. He didn't want to be talked down to anymore, to be told that things would be taken care of for him. "Yes," he said after a while, even though that wasn't quite true.

"Good, then I'll go first," Jewel said.

"No," James said, putting a hand out to stop her. "I will."

With his insides trembling like jello, he stepped through the mirror.

CHAPTER TWELVE

For the first time, he landed on his feet. The wind buffeted him, causing James to squint his eyes tightly and threatening to blow his small frame over, but he had landed on his feet. He smiled, he was getting better at this.

They were on some sort of rocky outcropping by the ocean, the terrain under them hard slabs of gigantic rock with sprigs of little green plants sprouting through them. Below them waves crashed mightily against the rocks. The smell of the water was fresh, and clean, and on the horizon the sun was setting, a dark ember, orange in a cloudless sky.

"Do you know which story this is?" James asked. Jewel and Adlan were scanning the horizon. Behind them lay nothing but land.

Adlan smiled, stepping back from the edge. "I'm going to let you two figure out which one this is. It shouldn't take long. I'm going to find a good seat."

The roar of a cannon broke through the howling wind and brought the three of them back to the edge of the cliff. Below them on the ocean two large ships came into view, one chasing the other, their sails billowing in the wind, traveling fast toward land. A second cannon shot rang out and a small puff of smoke came from the ship doing the chasing.

"Ah," Jewel said, "I think it's Chester the Molester. Careful James, there's going to be a crash here soon."

The front ship never even slowed as it approached the shore, ramming its keel into the rocks below with the sound of a fierce crash. From the top of the deck a figure dressed all in black ran toward the shore, leaping up onto the rocks and climbing with a fierce determination. As he climbed, the second ship slammed straight into the back of the first one, splitting it down the middle. Another figure ran across the top of the decks, hopping over debris, and began climbing after the first one.

"You'll want to back up, James," Adlan said. "Though it should be a good show." He picked up James in his strong arms and set him high on a boulder, helping Jewel up and then pulling himself up to sit beside them.

From the lip of the cliff a figure sprang up, and James gasped as he saw what it was. Standing as tall as a human and dressed in a ragtag cross between pirate gear and armor was the largest mouse that James had ever seen. He walked on his back legs like a human, and as James watched he pulled a large saber from his belt and held it deftly in his paws, taking a few practice swipes in the air and then standing at the ready as the other figure bounded over the ledge.

"Halt, brigand," the pursuer shouted. This figure was larger than the mouse, it was a ferret, and he too stood on his back legs and brandished a sword. He wore fancier armor, though; the fabric was finer and not frayed in the way that the mouse's was. "My wrongs will be avenged."

"Your wrongs?" The mouse said with a lopsided grin, "truly, Malthusias, 'twas I who was wronged. Your wife was so terrible in bed that *I* should be angry at *you*. I've never had a colder fish lie under me."

The ferret hissed and swung broadly at the mouse. "You have no honor, Chester, and no breeding to back you. I will be high praised to stomp your existence off this world once and for all."

Chester blocked the sword and sprang back with ease, the smile still on his face. As he circled around the ferret James got a good look at the other side of Chester's face. His one eye was covered with a black eye patch, a scar peeking out from under it. "Is honor ignoring your wife's needs and desires while you go running off with your chambermaids? If so then you can keep your honor. Oh yes," he said at the incredulous look the ferret gave him, "your wife's mouth was quite busy both during and after the act, I know a great many things about you."

The ferret charged at the mouse, swinging his sword low.

Chester jumped nimbly over the blade and cut back at him, catching him on the shoulder and causing Malthusias to stumble. The mouse went on the offensive with the ferret down on one knee, delivering a flurry of attacks that the ferret scrambled to defend. With one final slash to the side, the mouse disarmed his opponent, sending the ornate blade flying over the edge of the cliff.

"Yield, Malthusias, you have lost this day," Chester said, holding the tip of his blade to the ferret's throat.

"What are you going to do, kill me?" Malthusias asked, his paws raised in the air, his chest heaving as he tried to catch his breath.

Chester lowered his sword and stepped toward the cliff, turning his back to the defeated ferret. "You destroyed your ship coming after me, but I hold you no ill will, despite your previous treatment of me. Why don't you travel to King Ramus? It shouldn't be more than a few days' walk, and he will give you passage home."

Malthusias jumped to his feet and charged the mouse with his arms outstretched. "I'll drag you to hell instead!" he shouted, leaping at Chester.

With a deft duck and turn Chester tripped the ferret, using his own momentum to catapult him over the edge of the cliff down to the waters below. The ferret gave a surprised shriek as he fell, and Chester looked away before he hit the ocean.

"What a pity," Chester said, "it didn't have to end that way."

"As if you would rather have yourself down there," Jewel said as she climbed down the rock. Chester turned quickly, his blade raised. When he saw the girl he grinned and sheathed his sword.

"Jewel, what a treat it is to see you here. Did you come to finally claim the night of sensuous passion I promised to you so long ago?" Chester said, sweeping her up in his arms and trying to kiss her, his whiskers brushing her face.

She deftly slipped out of his grasp, smiling as she ducked away from him. "And that's why we call you Chester the Molester. No, I haven't come for that."

The mouse frowned and threw a theatrical hand to his forehead. "Oh, the hurt, it's like a thousand arrows burying themselves in my amorous heart! Truly you wrong me, I molest none," he grinned and winked at her, "that don't desire it."

Adlan jumped down from the rocks and clapped the mouse on his armored shoulder. "Hey mouse, I haven't seen you in a dragon's age, how have you held up?"

Chester smiled up at the hulk towering over him. "Is this a walking, talking mountain? What wizardry is this?"

"Chester, we have someone else for you to meet, he's actually the reason that we're traveling through here," Jewel said. "This is James."

Chester turned to James and ran a hand over his hair. His paw felt scratchy and warm. "Hey there, kid. What story did you come from? Is it a new one?"

"I'm not from a story," James said, "I just need to get out of here so I can help my dad. Jewel and Adlan are helping me."

Jewel took Chester aside for a moment and whispered into his large pink ears. The mouse's one red eye opened and his mouth dropped before coming back and kneeling before James. "My liege, I apologize. I didn't know, please forgive me mussing up your hair. Truly it won't happen again."

"I didn't mind it," James said. "We're trying to find a page that's been stolen so I can get home."

"A page has been stolen?" Chester's eyebrow contracted, the mischevious twinkle in his eye disappearing. "That's unprecedented. Who would dare alter the stories?"

Jewel placed a hand on Chester's shoulder softly. "It's Gladhands. I was in one that got changed," she shivered violently at the memory. "Luckily James heard my cry and changed it back."

Chester's face paled under his fur. He looked off to the distance across the ocean, fingering the hilt of his sword. "He won't be easy to find. I stopped traveling through the stories awhile ago, I kept getting lost in stories I didn't know. Some of them are pretty dark. What do you propose?" Chester asked.

"First things first, we have to get James back to his world, which means we have to find Gladhands and get back the page he took."

Chester stared in disbelief. "You're actively looking to find that monster!?" His open-mouthed look of shock then twisted into a manic sort of smile. "A suicide mission it is, then!" he said. "Count me in!"

"You don't have to come," James said, "if you don't want to."

The mouse knelt down and placed one hand upon his shoulder. "My liege, 'tis a matter larger than I. There is no other choice. I am coming with you, and should a blade need someone throwing themselves on it, I will gladly offer my body."

"Where is the doorway to the next story? I can never remember," Jewel said.

"Oh, we'll have to do a bit of walking for that. It's in a grove outside of King Ramus' castle. We might as well get going, it's getting on toward night time and it's a fair ways away."

*****

As they walked Chester pulled a small lute out of his bag and began to strum a tune, humming and singing alternately to pass the time as they walked away from the coast inland. The terrain under them changed from a rocky cliff to soft green meadow, the grass becoming long and full. As the sun fell and the earth got darker little lights began to shine around the hills, blinking on and off.

"Fireflies!" James said with a smile. "They look so beautiful."

Adlan cleared his throat loudly. "Ain't no fireflies. Them's fairies, and you'd be well off to stay away from them."

"My dear Adlan," Jewel said, "is there a species in the stories that you don't hate?"

"I don't hate fairies, I've just learned my lesson to stay away from them is all. Dangerous creatures."

"Oh, but you're so big and strong," Jewel said, adopting a simpering and overly feminine tone to her voice, "how could a little fairy ever get the best of you?" She petted his arms gently, pouting up at him. James laughed.

Adlan cocked an eye at her and drew his arm away. "You of all people should know that strength doesn't come with size, not in these worlds."

"What's the story with the fairies?" James asked.

"As you know, I used to do a fair bit of traveling between the stories myself," Adlan said. "One day I come across a grove with this beautiful little lake, waterfall cascading down into it, mossy rocks all around. Just a picturesque place, right? I remember there were these little purple flowers growing all over the ground. Well, over the top of the pond fluttered all these little fairies."

"Sounds magnificent," said Chester.

"Oh, it was pristine, just a gorgeous place. I took off my boots and stuck my feet into the water, and I think that was the most relaxed I've ever been. As I'm resting the waterfall separates, like it was a curtain, and this one fairy, larger than the rest, human-sized, steps out. Now, I've seen my share of attractive ladies before, so take my word when I say that this one was the prettiest I had ever seen."

Chester's eye swiveled around to Adlan and he quieted; the man had his complete attention. "Could you describe her to me?"

Adlan smiled. "Fiery red hair, smooth skin creamy as butter. And she had these great giant..."

"Adlan!" Jewel said, interrupting him. "May I remind you there's a child here?"

"I'm not a child!" James said, indignant.

"Eyes!" Adlan finished. "I was going to say these great giant beautiful green eyes. Anyway, she comes up to me, right, not even saying a word, and just starts putting her hands all over my face and body, smiling at me the entire time. Now here I am, thinking that I'm just about the luckiest man in the world, feeling more and more relaxed, drowsy even. Well, she worked some sort of magic on me because I fell asleep and when I woke up I was in a field miles away, fairies nowhere in sight, and I was completely naked!"

James and Jewel burst out laughing, causing Adlan to blush. Chester, however, did not look as entertained. "It's not funny," Chester said, "a woman using her feminine mystique on a man and then leaving him vulnerable like that. It's happened once or twice in my day. I feel for you, Adlan, she had no right to do that."

"Damn right, she didn't," Adlan said. "I had to walk to the nearest castle and find out just where in the hell I was. They gave me some clothes, but the look on the chambermaid's face when I showed up like that, I've never been so embarrassed."

"Ah, I'm sure she'd seen it all before," Chester said, "chambermaids are notoriously promiscuous. Come to think of it, I haven't yet met a chambermaid I didn't like."

James was struck by a sudden thought. "Are all fairies women?" he asked.

"No," Chester said, "but they are almost all tricksters. Comedy aside, Adlan is right to tell you to guard yourself when dealing with a fairy. Carefully think on everything that they say. They're not bad, they just like to have a joke, and their sense of humor doesn't align with most."

"Well, every time I've had run-ins with fairies they've been wonderfully helpful," Jewel said.

"Oh, come off it. You just like to think the best of everyone," Adlan said, giving her a playful little push.

Chester stopped walking altogether and the rest of the group turned. His face was drawn tight, somber and serious. "I just had a thought. Stealing a page isn't like changing the stories. To change a story would require an immense amount of power, there are few that could do it, but stealing a page is something else entirely. It would mean altering something on the outside." He turned and held a hand to James' shoulder. "James, has anything been happening in your world?"

"What are you saying, Chester?" Jewel asked, her brow furrowed.

The truth was something *had* been changing, and James knew it. "I really do need to get back," he said, ignoring the question.

Chester nodded, not pressing the point further, and they continued on. The previous joviality they had felt all but vanished as the sun finished its descent and they made their was across the field.

*****

"What was that?" Chester said, holding out his hand to stop the group. They were approaching a forest; the light was getting dark enough that they had to squint to see beyond ten feet. The fairies in the distance twinkled like little orange stars. "Quiet, I think I hear something."

In the silence the rest of the group could hear it as well. A low shuffling, almost a scraping sound, came from the forest. It was unnatural, otherworldly, and it made the hairs on the back of James' neck stand up.

"Are there normally creatures in the forest?" James asked, his voice quavering more than he would have liked. Between having seen dragons and talking mice already, James wasn't going to rule out the possibility of anything being down there. For the umpteenth time since he had started coming into the stories, he wished he were back home, tucked under his blankets all warm and safe.

Chester walked forward, unsheathing his sword. He knelt and pawed at the grass, pulling it aside until he could reach the dirt underneath. Scooping up a handful of the black earth, he rubbed it over his blade. Adlan mimicked him, rubbing the stuff over his large hand and a half sword.

"What are they doing that for?" James whispered into Jewel's ear.

"Dulling the shine," she said and then hushed him when he

131

tried to press further. "Stay here, let the adults deal with this."

Chester and Adlan worked well together, they pressed forward with their backs to each other, their swords held at the ready as Jewel followed.

Despite his fear, the sting of being excluded bothered James more. He was the one who had snuck by the dragon, wasn't he? James stood for most of a single second before disobeying the order to stay still. If something was going to happen, he wanted to be a part of it. He followed at a distance.

They entered the forest, careful with their footing to not disturb the dried leaves underfoot. The scraping sound was getting louder, accompanied by a wet slurping noise that sent shivers down the back of James' spine. It was a grotesque sound, and though he couldn't place exactly what it was, he felt his stomach turn sour just listening to it. Though they were shrouded in darkness, James was sure that his face was rapidly turning green.

They made it to the edge of a clearing, staying well hidden behind trees, and finally saw what was making the noise. In a grove below them a figure lay on his back, legs pale in the growing moonlight. Something was hovering over his face, its back arched. The thing seemed to pump its head and emit the slurping sound. As it shifted and the moonlight fell upon the inert figure, James' eyes widened. He knew in an instant what it was, the pointed ears and thin, waif-like form gave it away. An elf lay in the grove, struggling under *something*.

Every minute or so the elf's legs kicked on the ground, scraping at the leaves and twigs, but he couldn't dislodge himself. Every struggle seemed to get weaker. James peered closer. It looked as though there were tentacles coming out from the thing wrapping themselves tighter and tighter around the figure on the ground.

"What is it?" James whispered.

Jewel gave a start and then glared at him. "I told you to stay back."

"I don't know, but it's not something that belongs in my story," Chester replied, standing out from behind the tree. He raised the blade to shoulder height and crouched before sprinting out into the clearing.

The cloaked thing, the shadow with tentacles, hissed as it saw the mouse coming and rose up, releasing the elf. Whatever it was, it stood tall, dressed in a flowing black robe. Chester gasped as he saw its head, stumbling back even before completing his charge. The head looked like an octopus, with great black orbs bulging out of moist skin. Where a mouth should have been was instead a tangled mess of tentacles, all reaching toward the mouse. In the middle of the tentacles mashed a bloody little beak, snapping together.

"Oh no," Jewel said, "I know what that is. Quick, we've got to help."

Chester seemed to be frozen in place, his sword held loosely, as he looked into the eyes of the slowly advancing creature. Though it was the most absurd thing that he could have done in that situation, Chester dropped his weapon and his mouth hung slack, his shoulders slumping.

Jewel opened her mouth and began to sing, the notes low and melodic. The effect was instantaneous, the beast stopped advancing on the frozen mouse and its head began to droop, its eyes drooping shut. Just as James was sure it was over, the thing seemed to catch itself as it was falling asleep and shook its head, snarling at Jewel and reaching its tentacles toward her. Jewel's song may not have affected the creature, but the distraction allowed for Chester to snap out of whatever trance he had been placed in enough to pick up his sword and swing it at the tentacled beast. His aim was true, and he clipped the thing straight through its neck, the head lopping off and falling to the ground with a thump. The body didn't seem to get the message at first, its hands still grasping toward Jewel, but eventually that too fell down.

"What the hell was that?" Chester asked, wiping green blood from his sword. "That shouldn't be in my story, I haven't even seen those while traveling."

"I have," Jewel said, her face pale. She stared down at the severed head, its tentacles twitching and the beak gaping. "Though I've never seen one above ground. It's called a takoin, and be thankful that we only had to deal with the one. They're normally cave dwellers, they like the underground, the dark. They nest together, sometimes in packs up to fifty or more." She pulled out a small knife from Adlan's waist and kneeled by the head, using the tip of the knife to push aside the tentacles of its face. "The eyes hypnotize you, holding you in place for your fear. If you ever encounter one while you're alone, count yourself among the dead. They hypnotize you and pull you close with these tentacles, which are the strongest muscles they have. Then they latch onto your face, you see this beak in the middle? It's hard as a diamond and sharp as a razor. It'll split through your skull within a few moments, and its spit is an acid that drips into your brain, liquifying it so that the takoin can then suck out your brains."

"How do you know all this?" Adlan asked. James could barely believe his eyes, but he thought that he saw the big man shivering with fright. "I mean, I've done my fair share of wandering, but never down to places where these things could live. Those sound like bad stories."

Jewel smiled at him. "A woman has to have some secrets, now doesn't she?"

James knelt down at the side of the elf. The skin on the body was still warm. There was no doubt that he was dead, there was a great hole in his forehead from where the takoin had been feasting on his brains. The elf was dressed in a green tunic, a sword and knife on his belt, the scabbards of both emblazoned with an insignia of a dragon. "Chester, are there elves in your story?" James asked, unbuckling the belt from the dead elf and attaching it to his own waist. If things were going to continue this way, it would be better for him to be armed than not.

"None," Chester said, eying the sword that James had picked up. "Are you sure you'll be able to handle that? It looks sharp."

"Besides, James, aren't we going to get you the Arbiter? You shouldn't need a sword, we'll be here to protect you," Jewel said.

James frowned, tapping his foot against the ground. He was really getting sick of the way Jewel was treating him. "You know, Jewel, I seem to remember that it was *me* who saved *you* in your own story. I can make decisions for myself, and I'm deciding that until I find your stupid Arbiter sword I'm going to wear this one. Chester, I think it would be best if you and Adlan would teach me a few things, I would rather not be completely defenseless. Would you be willing?"

Adlan smiled, some of his color returning. "Of course we would."

Chester kicked the body of the takoin a few times. "What the hell are these things doing in *my* story? My story is supposed to be a lighthearted tale about the amorous exploits of *me*, not some horror story about these tentacled face suckers."

"Gladhands." Jewel said. "It's got to be his influence. He's gaining ground, allowing all the darker elements of the stories to grow stronger, to expand out and infect others with their presence. Something caused the balance to shift."

A look of sudden concern crossed Chester's face. "We need to warn the castle, they can't be left defenseless against these things."

Adlan smiled. "I thought you hated royalty. You better be careful, Chester, or you're in danger of becoming a decent character."

Chester turned. "I don't like King Ramus, that's true. He's a bit of a pompous ass, but I do have to admit that I'm quite partial to Melinda."

"Who's Melinda?" James asked.

"The king's daughter," Jewel whispered into his ear with a smile.

CHAPTER THIRTEEN

It was not a far walk from the end of the forest to the castle, though the darkness of the night made it seem much longer. They jumped at every shadow and walked with their weapons drawn. Adlan showed James how to smear dirt over his new blade and whispered advice, though most of it boiled down to 'stab them before they attack you.'

The castle itself was only visible from where it obscured the stars. There were no lights on the ramparts nor in the windows, and though it rose high, with spires piercing up into the air, it looked foreboding.

"I don't like this," Chester said as they walked across the open drawbridge. "The king may not be my friend, but he runs a livelier castle than this. Where are the guards? Where are the lights? Why isn't the drawbridge up for the night? It seems a deserted place."

It was surreal. Though the large ramparts still stood and the walls were intact, they didn't come across a single person when entering the castle. Chester led them through an archway and up a set of stairs, their footsteps echoing off the bare walls. A cool wind blew past them and James shivered. "Is it always so cold in your story?"

Chester shook his head. "The story centers around the conflicts that my amorous ways generate. It's a summer story." He unsheathed his sword and motioned for James and Adlan to do the same. "Something's gone wrong, I don't like it." His furry face was scrunched in worry, the brow above his one good eye furrowed.

They walked up another flight of stairs and wound around a corridor before they got to a section overlooking the king's hall. Chester motioned for them to stay in the shadows as he snuck forward, walking on all fours as quietly as only a mouse can.

Chester peeked over the side of the balcony and immediately withdrew, the skin under his fur paling and his breath coming quickly. "They're here," he said. "The bastards are here."

Before Jewel could stop him James ran forward and looked for himself, almost immediately wishing that he hadn't. There were six of them down there, the takoin, and a pile of bodies so thick he couldn't see the floor. The takoin were walking over them like they were carpet, stopping to suck occasionally at a body. Blood ran into the cracks of the stone floor, spider-webbing out. In a dark sort of equality the king was laid right alongside his page.

Chester flexed his hand into a fist, rocking back and forth. "I'm going down there, we have to clear these demons out."

Jewel grabbed hold of him and cradled his head to her breast, shushing him in a motherly way. "You wouldn't last two minutes down there. They're barely affected by my song, and the moment they saw you they would entrance you until they could suck out your brains."

Chester looked as though his one eye was on the verge of tears. "Melinda's down there, she's among the bodies. I can't just leave her there."

"It's okay, it's okay," Jewel said, "they're altering the stories, but there's no one saying that we can't alter them back. This just confirms what I've been saying all along; we need to defeat Gladhands and we can set all these stories back to their right way. Then Melinda will be back and your story will be just as it was."

"Defeat him?" James asked. "I thought we were just trying to get me home. I've met Gladhands, I don't know that we *can* defeat him."

Adlan stepped forward and placed a hand upon Jewel's shoulder. "I'm never one to shy away from a fight, missy, you know that. But let's be honest with ourselves, you're not just planning on getting James back to his world, are you?"

Her eyes flashed with anger. She glanced over the side of the balcony and then ducked down again. "I really don't think now is the appropriate time to have this conversation. Let's just get to the next story, we need to keep moving. Chester, where is it?"

Chester swallowed hard. "It's in Melinda's bedroom."

"Perfect. Where is her bedroom?"

With a paw that was slightly trembling, he pointed down across the king's hall to an archway. The takoin were feasting mightily in front of it. "There," he said.

*****

They walked down a winding staircase to the king's hall, keeping to the shadows behind pillars, trying to plug their ears against the slurping sound that echoed off the walls. Chester led them, scowling at the takoin as they feasted upon the royalty.

James had never felt his heart beat quite as hard or as fast as when they moved by the takoin. They were within twenty feet, though each seemed blissfully unaware of the group as they sucked the brains out of their victims. Disturbingly, at such a close distance James heard something even worse than the sucking. Each takoin emitted a low moan, a little sigh of pleasure every time it slurped a little more. It was evident how they relished the taste of the brains.

At the archway, as Jewel and Adlan hurried through, Chester held back. "What are you doing?" Jewel whispered. "We need to keep moving!"

Chester was still as stone, his paws gripping the handle of his sword tightly. Following the line of his vision, James saw what he was staring so intensely at.

One of the takoins had moved onto a new victim, a young blonde woman of extraordinary beauty. She lay limp, unresisting, as the takoin's tentacles slowly wrapped around her head.

"She's dead, Chester," Jewel said. "We have to keep moving. Besides, it's not like you truly love any of these women."

His one eye flashed to her in anger and his lips curled in a scowl. With a snarl he pushed her back and drew his sword, charging headlong into the pile of bodies toward the takoin.

James watched it all as though he were dreaming, it was too fast, too drastic of an action taken. The mouse bounded over bodies and swung hard with his sword, clipping the takoin in the back as James just watched wide-eyed.

The movement startled the others and they dropped their respective meals, moaning low and shambling toward the mouse. Chester had succeeded in freeing Melinda, but she hung ragged in his arms, a slimy pink substance running from a hole in her head.

"Adlan, come help me," Jewel said, running out of the tunnel.

"I'll be right there," the big man called, his face pale and sheepish. James watched as he disappeared down the tunnel.

Jewel opened her mouth and sang as loud as she could, taking the takoin by surprise. The moment's hesitation she caused allowed for Chester to stab his curved saber into the heart of one of the takoin, though the rest recovered quickly.

Tentacles reached out toward both Jewel and Chester as the five remaining takoin advanced. James watched as they moaned and locked eyes with their prey, both Jewel and Chester dropping their weapons as they became hypnotized.

James looked back down the tunnel where Adlan had disappeared. It was clear he wasn't coming back. With a few deep breaths, his hands shaking violently, he ran out behind the takoin's lines and stabbed upward into one of them with as much power as his arms could muster.

The blade slid up into the takoin's soft body, felling one, but the rest turned upon him in an instant. They moaned and stared, their eyes turning a bright shade of red, and James backed up slowly. He felt afraid, though the sensation was muted, and not immobilizing. Why wasn't he affected the same way?

The armor! It glowed over his heart, the warmth and light shielding him from the full strength of the takoin's hypnotizing eyes. A rush of confidence filled him and he snaked forward and thrust his little sword into the belly of another takoin.

His confidence faded quickly, however, as the creatures stopped trying to immobilize him and simply spread their tentacles toward him, advancing slowly. They were still three to one, and much bigger than he was. He held his sword up, the glow of his armor fading and the fear finally beginning to grow within him.

Things looked bad, Jewel and Chester had yet to snap out of their stasis and James was rapidly being backed into a corner. Trying to display more courage than he felt, he slashed the little elven sword this way and that, attempting to keep the takoin at bay, but still their tentacles came closer.

A sudden and loud bellow echoed through the hall, a war-cry of epic proportions. Just as the takoin were about to snatch James into their tentacles, a blur of red and brown appeared behind them, swinging a gigantic sword across the three of them.

James' eyes widened. Adlan *had* come back!

The large warrior made short work of the three takoin, chopping them apart with great cleaving strokes and leaving them in a bloody green pile on the ground.

"Adlan!" James said. "I thought you had abandoned us."

"Would that be anything a great warrior would do?" he said,

wiping the blood off of his blade.

"You're a coward, Adlan," Jewel said, coming to her senses as soon as the creatures were dead. "Admit it. You only came when you knew you could finish the fight quickly."

"I admit nothing except heroics," Adlan said, beaming at the three of them.

Chester knelt alongside Melinda's drained body, cradling her to his chest. The other three sobered when they looked upon the mouse grieving. After a few moments he laid her back down, closing her eyes and arranging her limbs in a respectable fashion. He said nothing, simply motioning back toward the archway.

The stairs down led to a bedroom that was decorated in pink. A large bed stood in the center of the room and a vanity sat off to one side with many different sizes of silver hairbrushes laid out, along with multiple bottles of spray perfume. Chester tried to speak when they first entered, cleared his throat, and then tried again. "This was Melinda's room. I'd ask that you treat it with the respect it deserves."

"It *is* Melinda's room," Jewel said, her countenance suddenly fierce. In the low, pink shaded light of the room her eyes danced crazily, and James cocked one eye up at her. "She's coming back, we just have to drive Gladhands back to his own story, to put him back in his place," Jewel said.

"Why are you so keen on fighting Gladhands?" Adlan asked. "Let's have it, right here and now. I told you, I'm all for fighting, but I won't go without all the details. I won't be used like that."

Jewel brushed the hair back from her head and scowled at them all. Her shoulders were hunched up, she looked like a big cat hissing at shadows. "We're wasting time, we have to keep moving."

James stepped forward and crossed his arms. There was a weariness that had settled in his shoulders, it was nowhere near exhaustion, but it put him into an introspective and slightly irritable mood. "No, I think Adlan is right. You're hiding something, we need to know what it is before this goes any farther."

"Jamie, do you want to get back to the real world?" Jewel said. "I'd have thought you would be keen to, what with all your father is going through."

"That's not my name," James said. "Who are you, really? A simple princess in a story wouldn't care about that. It doesn't seem like many of the other characters do, present company excluded," he said, holding up his hands in an inoffensive gesture toward Adlan and Chester. The mouse was too busy looking forlornly at the bed and running the silk sheets through his paws to pay any attention, but the giant shrugged.

Jewel turned her back on them and took a few deep breaths. When she turned back around her face looked much more calm, blank even. It looked neutral, mask-like. James didn't like it one bit.

"You're right," she said, spreading her arms. "You're right. I'm not just a simple princess. Certain characters get used a lot in different stories. It gives them power beyond just the story they're in. That's part of how Gladhands is so strong. He's in more and more stories," she paused and bit her lip, "Your father is very dear to me, I have a link with him that only one other person in the stories does. Gladhands. So while everyone else was content to just continue to play out their parts as they had been created, I knew that I couldn't. I went to spy on Gladhands, to find out how strong he had gotten. I got caught, and he put me back in one of my stories and disabled the only way I had to fight. I was trapped, until I called out to you, James."

James crossed his arms, his eyebrows scrunched together. "But how were you able to? It never happened before that a character reached out into the real world to me."

The mask on Jewel's face was gone in a flash, a slight smile creeping onto her face. She tried to hide it, the corners of her mouth tried to keep it in check, but it shone through. It was not a completely happy smile, James might have been

147

imagining it, but when Jewel smiled at this he swore he saw something deeply sad there. It was confusing to see someone simultaneously joyful and sad at the same time.

"You and I also have a link, James. It allowed me to break the ground between our world and yours, and in doing so I inadvertently showed the way to the ogre and the child." she said.

His face went from open-eyed confusion to curiosity, and gradually it darkened. As he made the connection he began to grind his teeth together, to breathe deeper. "Did Gladhands follow your path? Is that how he is affecting my father? Did you do this to him? DID YOU?!" By the end he was shouting at her, his face hot with rage. His hands were balled up into fists, he wanted to strike out, to destroy.

Jewel knelt and ran a hand along his face. Her touch soothed his temper, if only a little. "Hush, James. No, Gladhands did not follow me." She took a deep breath and bit her lip. "Gladhands is...something else. Gladhands and I are different than your average characters, because we're not only written here, in multiple different stories, but we're also something outside of here. Your father is in trouble; it's not just the stories that Gladhands is changing, it's him."

James tapped his toes together and bit his lip. "You never meant to simply send me back through the page, did you? I get the feeling that you've got something else in mind."

She wouldn't look at him. "It's true," she admitted. "I never meant to simply send you back there. You have to understand that if we just did that the problem wouldn't be solved. A part of your father is broken, and I think that if we defeat Gladhands we can fix it. And you have to play an integral part in that."

"Why me?" James asked. "I'm just a kid." He felt ashamed as soon as the words left his mouth. He knew he was being selfish, but this was all a lot for him to handle. Brain eating octopi? Ninety-nine point nine percent of people *never* had to deal with that in their lives. Ogres and takoin and mad surgeons were all a lot of fun when he read about them, but to actually experience their horrors first hand? How could they ask such a thing of him?

Jewel put a hand on his shoulder. "Your father wrote you into a lot of stories as well. You're not just any kid, you have power in these stories that you haven't even begun to grasp, and I think that you and I together can put Gladhands back into his own story and seal him there."

Scowling, James felt an awful large weight on his shoulders, as though Jewel had just placed a physical burden there. If it was true, and Gladhands was affecting his father's worsening well-being, then there was no way that he could turn his back on all this, whether he liked it or not.

Adlan placed a gruff hand on James' shoulder. "You won't be alone, laddie, I'll be right there alongside you."

Chester stepped forward as well and wiped at his red eye. "I've got my own reasons for helping defeat this monster, but I'll fight alongside you just the same. We're not just fighting for our stories any more, we're fighting for all the stories."

James nodded once, confidence in himself growing. "All right, Chester, how do we get to the next story then?"

Chester walked to the side of the room and opened a half-sized door. "Through Melinda's closet."

James peered inside. It was stuffed to the brim with clothes. "Are you sure we'll be able to get through there?"

"Oh, the great lummox there will probably be in for a bit of a squeeze, but once you're at the back we should pop out in the next story," Chester said, pawing aside the rows of dresses and skirts and climbing to the back of the dark closet.

James climbed his way through after him. "Why this closet? Is there any significance to where the stories synch up?"

Chester stopped midway through and flashed him a mischievous grin. "Well the king almost catches Melinda and me together in my story, I have to hide naked in this closet to keep him from finding me. So that might be it, otherwise I'm not really sure."

Adlan let out a large guffaw and then held a hand over his mouth. He was the last to attempt the climb. Chester was certainly right, he didn't have the easiest time fitting, but by the end of the closet he fell through just like the rest of them.

CHAPTER FOURTEEN

James fell hard onto a cold wooden floor. Looking around at his surroundings, he saw that he was in a bedroom again, though this one was vastly different from the princess's that they had just come through. The walls were bare and dirty, the bed composed of just a single mattress bereft of even a sheet. There were bits of food molding on the ground, and dust covered everything. No pictures decorated the wall, there was no dresser nor any other bit of furniture aside from the bed. Still, something seemed remarkably familiar about the place. "Where is this?" James said in a whisper.

Jewel's eyes narrowed and her face grew pale. She held a single finger to her lips. "I'm not sure."

They walked across the wooden floor to the door. Even though they were stepping slowly, the wood creaked alarmingly under them. They moved out into a long hallway. There were no lights to guide them, they had to feel their way along the walls. From out of the darkness the faint sound of a woman whispering reached their ears, though they couldn't exactly tell what it was that she was saying. At the end of the hallway they reached a flight of stairs going downward and followed it.

The back of James' neck tingled as he walked down the

stairs. "I know this place," he said in a hushed whisper. "This is my house, well, kind of." It was eerie how similar it was to his house. The layout was the same, he even correctly guessed which steps to avoid to not have them creak, but the furnishings were vastly different. There were no pictures of the family on the wall, no drawings that James had made in school, none of his toys. There weren't even the pictures of his mom; in his house in the real world there was a little shrine set up in homage to her. The whispering grew louder as they moved downstairs.

"It's your fault," it said. "It's all your fault. Had to have that last drink, didn't you? You should end it now, save yourself the pain. We all know how selfish you really are, but do something for everyone else. End it." The voice was low and serpentine, the sentence hissing along.

"Did you hear that?" Jewel asked. They moved down the hallway toward a cracked-open door. Light filtered around the edges, a thin and watery light that did no more than accentuate the darkness.

"Stay here," James said, "I'll check it out. I know this house." He walked down the hallway and slid his head through the door. When he saw the room his mouth opened in a silent gasp.

It was his father's office, but everything was changed. The

desk was backward, pushed up against the wall. There were no bookcases on the shelves and the big leather couch was gone. It was just a desk and a chair in the middle of the room. His father was sitting in it, hunched over, his spine curved at a painful-looking angle. The man looked small and dirty, wearing a stained white t-shirt and pajama bottoms with no shoes. James shifted around to get a better look inside the office.

"Think of your son," the snake-like voice hissed in the office. It took a moment for James to find the creature that was speaking. Floating above his father in tight circles was a translucent ghost, a shimmering specter who sneered at the man out of eyeless sockets. Every time it said something it floated down to perch right beside Patrick's ear. "You ruined your son's life. Think of how he must *hate* you. A boy really needs his mother, and you took that from him."

"I didn't mean it," Patrick said, his voice small and broken.

As he crept further into the office James noticed a full glass of amber liquid sitting in front of his father, the only thing on the desk. He moved around, the ghost seemed not to notice him, and saw how his father's eyes were rimmed red and trembling.

"It was the other driver's fault," Patrick pleaded, not looking at either the ghost or his son as he came into view.

"But who was it who was supposed to drive that night?" the

ghost hissed, floating upside down, its lips inches from Patrick's ear. "You know how she felt about driving in the winter. You said you'd drive, and then you got so drunk you couldn't."

His father picked up the glass and looked at it for a good minute or so before draining it down. As he set it back down on the table it filled itself again. "There, I've had my drink, now will you leave me alone?"

"But look at you now," the specter continued, "drinking on a Tuesday. Didn't you learn anything from your mistake? Quite the example that you're setting for your little one. Where is Jamie now? Probably choking to death and you won't be able to do anything about it because here you are, drinking on a Tuesday."

"Leave my dad alone!" James shouted, storming toward them. The specter wheeled up high in the air and hissed down at him before vanishing through the walls. Patrick still sat at the table, staring at the wall, his trembling fingers tapping the side of the full glass of scotch. James placed a hand on his father's arm. "Dad, are you okay?"

James recognized the look on his father's face, it was the same he had had right before James went back into the stories. That slack-eyed numb stare, lips slightly parted. The sour smell of the amber liquid wafted from him.

"Hey Jamie," Patrick said, not looking at his son. "Do you want me to read you a story? It's called 'Jamie and the Dragon.'"

"Dad, are you okay?" James asked again.

Patrick picked James up and sat him in his lap, still not looking at him, still numb, still slack-eyed. The sour smell was stronger, his father seemed soaked in it. "Why does everyone keep asking me that?" he said as his arms dropped back down to the chair.

James picked up his father's arms and tried to wrap them around himself, but the muscles wouldn't comply. They just dropped down to the chair every time he moved them. Behind Patrick James saw Jewel enter the room, her face taut and strained.

"Let's go, James," she said, pulling him down off his father's lap. "We should get out of this story, we need to keep moving."

"What's wrong with him? Why is he like that?" James asked, suddenly feeling very angry that this *thing*, not his father at all, just a *thing*, couldn't do anything but sit and stare at a wall. Jewel pulled him toward the door and he struggled out of her grasp, running back to his dad and kicking him as hard as he could in the shin.

Patrick just sat there, like he hadn't even felt it, staring at the wall with his glass full of amber liquid.

"Come on, James," Jewel said, pulling him back out into the hallway. Chester and Adlan stood quietly, their faces drawn, their eyes downcast.

When they were back in the hallway the sound of whispering returned, saying. "It's your fault, it's all your fault. Had to have that last drink, didn't you?"

"Why is he like that?" James said, so frustrated he was almost seeing red. "That's not a story at all, that's just him sitting there with a ghost."

"That's how the story was written," Jewel said, placing a hand on his shoulder.

He shrugged it off, he didn't feel like being touched right then. He wanted to be alone, to be miles away from anyone else. "What do you mean? You mean he would just write a scene of him and a ghost? That doesn't make sense."

Jewel nodded. "There's a lot of little fragments like that. Someone told him that it may help if he were to write those thoughts down. I don't think it did."

Hot, shameful tears sprang to James' eyes. He turned away from them, he didn't want them to see him cry. It was stupid, he hadn't cried openly since the funeral, so why was he crying now? A man doesn't cry. Only little children cry. "Is he broken?" James asked.

To his surprise, it was Adlan who responded. He pulled out

a handkerchief large enough to be a small blanket and handed it to James. "Just because a man's got problems like that don't mean he's broken. Just means he's got some things to be working out. You never see it in the stories, but lots of guys are like that after battle. Couple of the bloodier ones I've visited have whole contingents of men like that after seeing their friends get cut down by a dragon or an ogre. Ain't nothing to be ashamed of."

James nodded and blew his nose into the handkerchief before giving it back to Adlan. "Let's keep going. I don't want to stay in this story any longer than we have to. Do you know where the opening to the next story is?"

Jewel nodded. "I can guess. I haven't been in this particular story but a lot of these tend to have the same one." She led them to a half-sized door under the stairway and held it open for them.

"The basement? Really?" James asked. "There's nothing down there but some skiing equipment and lawn chairs."

"In your basement maybe, but keep in mind that this isn't *really* your house. This is the story's house. And it might not have been created exactly as it exists in your world."

They walked down the stairs, flicking the light on as they went. James could see what Jewel was talking about almost immediately. It wasn't his basement at all. Where there should have been storage crates and shelves with canning supplies there was bare concrete and a dirt floor. In the center of the floor rose a stone well, the old-fashioned kind that people hundreds of years before would have retrieved their water from.

"A well?" James asked. "We don't have a well down here."

Jewel nodded. "They seem to pop up here and there through your father's stories, always as a sort of focal point. Don't ask me what they mean."

Chester stepped to the side of the well and looked down. "Is that where the next story is?" Jewel nodded. "But you can't really expect us to climb down there, it's wet!"

"Chester, are you afraid of getting wet?" Jewel asked. "You have a ship in your story."

The mouse stood straight and adjusted his sword across his back. "I am certainly not afraid of getting wet. But I am wearing calfskin boots that I'm rather partial to."

Jewel laughed. "I doubt very much you'll hit the water. Would you mind giving me a hand?" With the mouse's assistance she climbed up to onto the lip of the well and allowed herself to fall in without a sound.

James gasped and peeked over the side. She was nowhere to be found in the shimmering, greasy water down below. "All right, if she can do this, so can I," he said, vaulting himself over the ledge. As the water approached he closed his eyes tightly and hoped that if Jewel was wrong, the well would at least be deep. He landed on his back on something soft and opened his eyes.

It was bright out. After the darkness of the last story it took a moment for James to be able to see, he had to allow his eyes to adjust. Adlan and Chester tore through the fabric of that story and landed next to him on the grass. It was surreal. Above them shimmered a disk of floating water, James could see up into his basement, but only through that disk.

They were standing in a grassy field, the sun was shining, birds were chirping merrily. It had the fresh and cool feel of a spring afternoon. Off in the distance James could hear music being played, a type of bluegrass that had him tapping his feet and smiling almost instantly.

"Well this is a pleasant change of pace," Adlan said as he stood and brushed himself off, "from moldy basements. Feels nice here in the sun."

"Ay, it does," Chester said, his one eye narrowed. James followed his line of vision. There was a group of people gathering in the distance, they seemed to be setting up some sort of gathering. There were colorful streamers being thrown through trees and people dancing about. "We seem to be in for a party. Jewel, do you know what story this is?"

"No, I don't," Jewel said, "It does seem rather too festive, though, don't you think? I'm not sure I like the look of it. We should find the next portal and be moving on soon. Something about this strikes me as wrong."

"What?" Adlan cried out. "We finally find a proper feast and you want to leave? I think we deserve a little break from this questing, how 'bout you, James?"

The smell of roast pork wafted from the group of people and James' mouth began to salivate. It felt like it had been days since he had eaten. "I think a look around wouldn't hurt anyone, don't you, Jewel?"

"I see maidens, what's more, I see unattended maidens," Chester said with a grin. He threw himself on his knees at Jewel's feet. "Oh can't we play, mum? Can't we play just a little bit?"

Jewel stifled a laugh behind her hand. "Oh, all right, let's see what the party is about. I want you all to be keeping a look out for trouble though, you never can tell with these things."

Chester and Adlan cheered and ran toward the party. James and Jewel took a little more of a leisurely pace, strolling across the grass. The sun felt warm and there was a light breeze blowing James' hair to one side. "He seems to be feeling better," James said. "Has he forgotten about Melinda already?"

Jewel looked after the mouse bounding away through the party and tucked a stray hair behind her ear. "That's his nature, he loves deeply, but his love burns through him quickly."

"What is it you're nervous about?" James asked. "It looks like any old party, maybe a bit old-fashioned dress-wise, but safe enough."

Jewel bit at her lip and scanned the crowd. Despite the spring feel of the day, her shoulders stayed tense and her hands balled up in fists at her sides. "Something just feels off about it," she said.

Everything seemed centered around a large wooden platform at the middle of the clearing. Someone had hung streamers of all colors from it that were blowing in the wind. All around people danced and played. Laughter filled the gaps the music left. A young big-toothed girl around James' age grabbed him by the hands and pulled him into a dance. They swung around and around, holding hands, and James was soon giddy with laughter himself. It was a light-headed and light-hearted feeling, and James felt the tight knot in his stomach begin to finally unwind a bit. Jewel sat off to one side, talking to no one, watching the crowd.

Chester danced with a buxom young red-haired woman with freckles splattered across her cheeks. She wore a dress below the knee and danced close to him. His paws slid their way liberally down around her backside as they swung in circles.

Adlan had invaded the dinner table, loading his plate up

high. The food they served smelled fresh, the entire spread loaded down with everything roast: roast pork, roast duck, roast chicken, as well as candied fruits and several different types of salads. "Don't know why they even had those here," Adlan said to James when he stopped dancing. "What with all that good meat to eat? They shouldn't have bothered."

Between the singing and the dancing James felt an almost intoxicating sense of happiness. He needed this, there had been too many bad stories he traveled through, he needed the time to just sit and rest his heels. He felt himself recharge. On the other side of the party he could see Chester and his red-haired woman sneaking off into the trees.

The music stopped abruptly, catching everyone's attention with its absence. A round little man had ascended the stage. He was colorfully dressed in red and yellow stripes, his cheeks flushed, and he carried a glass of wine in one hand and a length of rope in the other. He smiled and waved to the crowd as they cheered his arrival. He turned and set his wine glass down, swaying slightly, and then unwound the length of rope, throwing one part of it over a crossbeam mounted above the wooden platform.

"Hello, my people!" he shouted from on top of the platform. "As you know, today is decision day!" A great amount of cheering went up from the crowd.

Jewel left her vantage point and grabbed Adlan from off the dinner table. Her face was strained, and her eyes never left the little man on the platform above them. "Go get Chester, I think we might need him."

"There's a good chance that he's a might bit preoccupied," Adlan said with a wink. "I think I saw him go off yonder with a pretty young thing."

"Doesn't matter," Jewel said, "I feel like we'll need him here." Adlan shrugged and walked off toward the forest as Jewel grabbed James by the shoulder. "Stick with me, something's happening."

The rotund little man allowed the cheering to go on for a long time before finally raising his hands and calling for silence. "Now, our priests have been talking with the guilty one, and they tell us that he is finally ready to take his leave of us." Another round of cheering went up from the crowd. He let them shout, smiling largely in the glow of their cries.

"Burn him!" a voice in the crowd shouted. "Burn the guilty one!" This set off a few accompanying cries agreeing with him.

The round man waved his hands again. "We are a civil society, we don't burn people any more. Was that you, Bertrand? You're always calling for a burning. I think you've got a touch of pyromania in you." He smiled again at the crowd and they laughed at his joke. "No, we do this the humane way.

After all, Mike spent all this time setting up a gallows, it would be a shame to waste that. We'll just hang him and be done with it." A disappointed sigh went up from the crowd and the round man chuckled a bit. "One of these days, I promise you, we'll burn someone. But it's got to be a real special one, not like this trash here. Okay?"

James craned his neck. Everyone had crowded around the platform, blocking his view of what was going on. Adlan and Chester joined behind him, the mouse busy buckling his pants together, a red flush to his face. James tugged at Adlan's arms. "Can I sit on your shoulders?" he asked. Adlan nodded and picked him up with one massive hand and sat him on his back.

"I don't know that that's a good idea," Jewel said with a worried eye up toward James.

Adlan waved her away. "Oh come on, it won't hurt anything."

From atop Adlan's shoulders James towered over the crowd and was easily able to see the rotund man be joined by two others on the platform, one a colorfully costumed clown dancing up and down and the other a man wearing a black cloak pulled up over his head. The clown had a big red sad face painted over his own, and he rolled around the stage to the great delight of the crowd.

"All right," the round man said, "are we ready to hear

Patrick's confession?"

The crowd cheered. "Did he say 'Patrick'?" James asked.

Jewel shrugged her shoulders, her hand on the person in front of her, trying to get a better view. "I couldn't hear a thing."

The round man walked up to the man with the cloak over his head and pulled it off him with a theatrical flourish. James' jaw dropped and he felt as though he had just had the wind knocked out of him. Standing on the platform with his hands bound behind his back, looking very disheveled and unshaven, was his father. The crowd jeered and booed when he was unveiled to them.

"Dad?" James asked.

"What did you say?" Jewel said, "I can't hear a thing in this crowd."

"All right," the round man said, "let us be quiet and listen to the condemned's confession."

The crowd went silent and expectant as they turned to Patrick. His face was pale, but calm and composed as he stepped up to speak to them. "I've...I've been doing a lot of thinking," Patrick said, his voice initially trembling but gaining in confidence as he spoke. "You are all right to hate me. I hate me for what I allowed to happen. I come before you to say once and for all that it's all my fault. I ruined her life, and I

166

ruined my life," he looked down and cleared his throat, his voice warbling, "and I ruined our son's life. So it's come time for my atonement."

"James, get down here right now," Jewel said as she finally caught what was being said. "Adlan, put him down!"

"No," James said, "something's happening with my dad, I have to see what it is."

"I've come to the decision," Patrick said, his voice steadying, "that the world would be better off without me." The clown made exaggerated motions of crying to the crowd and they all laughed. The round man had busied himself tying the rope around Patrick's neck.

Jewel jumped up and grabbed James by his shirt, dragging him down off Adlan's back. He fell heavily to the ground with a thump, the wind being driven from his body. "What's going on? I don't understand, I have to get back up there and see what's happening."

She grabbed him roughly at the neck of his shirt and pulled him close with surprising ferocity. "You will do no such thing. I don't want you watching this, this is one of the bad stories, you understand? If Patrick didn't have Gladhands inside of him this story never would have happened."

James struggled against her. "That's my dad, I need to see," he said, trying to push her away and stand. A shock rocked his face to the side and a hot feeling of pain flashed on his cheek as she slapped him hard across the face. Tears sprang to his eyes.

"Now you listen to me, young man, keep your eyes on me," Jewel said. A great cheer went up from the crowd, muffled down where James was. "That isn't your dad. That's a character in one of his stories. You need to separate the two. Your father is back in your world, perfectly safe. Do you understand me?"

James nodded, his face feeling flushed. He scowled at the woman holding him, but quickly concealed it. His hands curled into fists and they itched, wanting to lash out, wanting to strike her back, to kick and gouge at her. Why was she doing this to him?

"Adlan!" Jewel called out, tugging on his leg. Adlan kneeled down to join them. "We need to get out of here fast. You have to help us locate the opening to the next story."

"I know where it is," Chester said, joining them. Another great cheer went up from the crowd all around them. "It's in the meadow where Erin took me. She's the red-haired girl," he said to the perplexed look Adlan gave him.

"Take us there," Jewel said. "Don't let James see."

Adlan picked up James bodily and carried him along into the woods, the cheering from the crowd growing faint. James kicked and struggled in the mountain's arms, but to no avail. "Where is it?" Adlan asked.

"It's in the base of this tree here," Chester said, pointing toward a great oak tree, so large that if they were to link arms and spread around it they wouldn't even come close to touching fingers. The roots were pulled up out of the ground, leading to something that resembled stairs down into the base right below the tree. Behind them the crowd had begun singing a joyful sounding tune. James couldn't see what was going on.

"Stop," James said, finally dislodging himself. "Stop, I have to catch my breath." He sat down hard in the grass. It was obvious that it had been his father, and that something very bad had happened to him up on that platform. The words Patrick had spoken to the crowd ran through his head. What had he to be guilty about? Why would he write a story like that?

"We should keep moving," Jewel said, "this isn't a good story."

His breathing came in great gasping heaves. It was overwhelming, and he was beginning to see darkness around the edges of his vision. "I need to know what's going on. My father would never have written a story like this. It's too dark, that's not who he is."

Jewel's face softened and she sat down beside him, rubbing his back with one hand. "I'm sorry I slapped you. I think you need to understand that this is all Gladhands' work. This is what he does, he gets inside someone and he just eats and eats until there's nothing left of the person. That story," she said, pointing back toward the party, "shows how far along he is. We need to save your dad, and we need to do it soon, otherwise every story will be like that."

"How much longer do we have?" James asked.

"The stories are getting darker," Jewel said, "I think we're getting closer."

Adlan clapped him on the back. "Cheer up there, laddie. We're going to save your dad, rest assured about that. No use looking grim, I mean, look at me. My dad died when I was very young; you at least have a chance to save your dad. Mine simply went out hunting one day and fell into a gorge. Alive one minute, dead the next."

"Your dad wasn't real!" James shouted in his face. He leaped to his feet, all his anger and his confusion coming to a head. "None of you! You're all just made up creatures, you don't matter. You think you have all these thoughts and memories and emotions but you don't! None of you do." He backed away from where they all stood, the hurt evident in their eyes. "You guys think you have any clue as to what I'm going through, fighting for my dad in a realm he created. Well you don't. You've never been real, you don't know what it's like." After a moment of looking into their stunned and hurt faces, he

170

turned and ran headlong into the forest, away from the oak tree, leaving them dumbfounded.

"James!" Jewel called out to him. "It's not safe! This isn't one of the good stories, you don't know what's out there!"

CHAPTER FIFTEEN

James ran until his lungs burned and his legs felt like jelly, not even paying attention to what direction he was headed. He only knew that he had to get away. This was all too much. How did they, or his father for that matter, expect him to work everything out when he was just a kid? He should be worrying about girls at school and Kenny the bully, not an otherworldly being that was destroying his father. How could they expect him to do this? His run slowed to a walk as he tired. The whole quest weighed upon him, the armor suddenly feeling heavy and constricting. With a snarl he tore it off him, desperate to be free from its heft, and threw it off into the trees.

"It's really unfair, isn't it?" A voice called out to him, putting words to his own thoughts. James looked around. The forest had grown dark and dense, shadows creeping through trees. A mist formed around his ankles, the sounds of frogs croaked in the distance. The sun must have gone down, though James hadn't noticed it. How had it gotten so dark so fast? A chill dried the sweat on his arms and goosebumps broke out. The area was bathed in moonlight, though it did little to illuminate all the shadows.

"Who said that?" James asked.

"Up here," the voice said. In the branches above his head James saw an oddly dressed man perched in the tree. He wore a red suit with a black tie, a top hat perched on his head, his limbs long and spindly. The man was smiling in an open and honest way. "Hello," he said. In a gloved hand he held a gold topped cane. "I said, 'it's really unfair, isn't it?'"

As James recovered from his mad sprint he sized up this new character. The man seemed innocent enough, if a bit loopy to be sitting up in a tree. In a way James was reminded of a curious cat in a fairy tale he had read once. "What's unfair?"

"Oh, lots of things. Life, to state a minor one. You're given all the free will in the world but such narrow confines to exercise it in." He smiled, his teeth reflecting the moonlight. When he talked he twirled his cane, flicking it between his fingers.

"What are you talking about?" James asked.

The man stood on his branch, holding the cane out for balance. He seemed remarkably nimble, tiptoeing around the tree like that. "I'm talking about *you*, James. Your choices. I'm talking about what no one else in these stories will. Don't you get tired of all the things they *won't* say to you?"

James furrowed his eyebrows. His neck was beginning to hurt staring up at the man at this angle. His anger faded down to a quiet simmer in the background, and he appreciated how

173

the man in the tree talked to him like he was a grown up. "How do you know who I am?" he asked. "Who are you?"

The man smiled again. "Oh, you're well known in these parts. But, I wonder, how well do you know yourself?"

James clenched his hands into fists. "I know myself quite well thank you very much. My name is James, I go to East View Elementary, my mother passed away two years ago, my father's name is Patrick. I have a cat named Hobbes who likes to sleep at the foot of my bed. Now, who are you?"

The man smiled and stood straight, allowing himself to tip precariously. He fell backward, the smile never leaving his face. As James put out a hand to stop him, the man caught hold of the tree branch by curling his foot around it and swung under the branch. He held himself there, dangling by one foot, the smile still on his face, upside down. Gravity didn't seem to affect him, his hat didn't fall off and his coat tails and tie stayed put. He held out one of his gloved hands and James shook it. "That's who you are in another life, that has no bearing on who you are here. Here you are...more. As for me, I go by many names, but you may call me Danghenam, very pleased to see you."

"Why would you say life is unfair?" James asked. He wanted to tip his head, to look at Danghenam in the proper orientation, but he resisted the urge. The man had been treating him like an equal, and he wasn't going to do anything childish to ruin that.

Danghenam shrugged the question away. "Oh, just starting a conversation. An unfair life seems to be something everyone can get on board with, but I see you're a man who likes specifics. Personally? I don't care for them. Vagaries have such a nice and fluid way about them, but to each his own, I guess. What I was really alluding to was your *burden* of *responsibility.*"

"I see," James said, though he wasn't sure that he actually did. This strange, upside-down man spoke in circles and it was difficult to parse meaning from his sentences. "What do you mean, the burden of my responsibility?"

Danghenam held his cane like a sword and waved it in front of him, his tongue sticking out of the corner of his mouth. From the tip of his cane a light trailed, as though he were drawing a picture on thin air. After a moment the picture became clear. It was his father, sitting in that old leather recliner in his office, half-full glass of amber liquid in his hand. "Your burden. It's unfair for you that your father cares more about his scotch, and his little stories, than he does for his own son."

"He does?" James asked. His stomach quavered. Love was something he had never thought of as questionable before. The very idea was earth shattering.

"Oh yes, oh yes. And now he's got this...*sickness* inside of him and looks to you to do something about it. What can you do? You're just a child, you shouldn't have to deal with that."

James felt very small. He wished that Jewel were here, or Adlan, or Chester. But they weren't, he had abandoned them. They were probably halfway back to their own stories by now. He was alone.

"Child," Danghenam said, "you're not alone, don't think that. They may have abandoned you, but I won't. You'll always have a friend in Danghenam. Always."

James stepped back with a start. "Can you read my mind?"

The upside-down man laughed. "Of course not. A mind is a person's sanctuary," he paused and seemed to consider something, "or prison cell, depending on how you look at it. But what I can do is read your face. Such an innocence about you. You shouldn't have to deal with your father's problems. And besides," he hooked his cane gently around James' neck and pulled him in close, his breath smelling like maggots and rotting leaves, "it was his fault that it happened, anyway. He knows that. He *invited* his sickness in. In many ways he *wants* it there, and that's something that he will never tell you, he might not even admit it to himself, but it's true. The suffering makes him feel...*absolved* from what he did. Do you understand?"

James unhooked the cane from around his neck. "No, I don't understand what you're saying at all."

Danghenam lodged his cane into the tree branch and flipped himself back right side up, landing on the ground near James. He put a hand to his hat. "Oh dear, it always takes a little getting used to, changing perspective like that. Well, I have a cabin not too far from here. I am wondering, since you are new to the area and we are fast becoming good friends, whether you would like to come back with me for a cup of tea?"

James looked toward the direction he had come from. He frowned. "I really should check on my friends, I kind of just left them there. Maybe then we can all have tea together? I can introduce you to them. I think you'd like them."

Danghenam curled an arm around James and knelt down. "My child, they are not your friends. They are like all the other adults, they seek to order you around and change your world for their own ends. Didn't you ever feel manipulated by them? Used, almost?"

James frowned, thinking hard. "Sometimes," he admitted.

Danghenam smiled. "Well, you'll never feel like that around me. And besides, those who you call your friends have already abandoned you. Let me show you," he said and then held his cane out again. He drew a box in the air and it came to life, showing Jewel, Adlan, and Chester all traveling through the entrance under the tree and into a different story. "You see? They never needed nor wanted you around for their quest. You were their burden, and it looks like they are happy to be rid of you."

A little niggling pain dug into James chest and his face soured. He felt like he had just been struck in the stomach. He took a few deep breaths and calmed down. "That doesn't mean they were happy to be rid of me, I mean, they're my friends."

"Are they?" Danghenam said. He waved his wand once more and the picture changed. It now showed James on one side, his fists balled up at his sides and his face beet red, shouting at the others.

"You're all just made up creatures, you don't matter. You think you have all these thoughts and memories and emotions but you don't! None of you do!" his own picture screamed, the sound of it blaring around him.

The little niggling pain in his chest grew slightly wider, sharper.

"Now tell me, is that the way friends talk to one another?" Danghenam said. "Don't worry, we'll never talk like that to each other. Come with me, let's sit and chat at my house. Have ourselves a cup of tea."

The pain in his chest intensified once more, and then with

the little sound of ripped jeans, it was gone. It was as though something tiny had torn a hole there. There was a small bit of nothingness that existed that had been filled not one day prior. There was no pain, indeed there was nothing at all, a cold nothingness. "All right, I'll come have some tea with you," he heard himself say as though from a great distance.

"Wonderful," Danghenam said, clapping his hands together. "It's just a short while this way."

Though James had quite the time pushing leaves and branches away from his face as they walked, Danghenam didn't seem to have any trouble with them. They all shied away from him, wilting backward and out of his way.

Beyond the trees they entered a little clearing with a table and chairs set up for them. Two cups and saucers were set out, and a kettle sat in the middle with a faint wisp of steam coming out from the spout.

"Where's your house?" James asked as he sat down in the chair.

Danghenam looked around, startled, his spiderleg fingers quivering in the air. "Oh my, I seem to have forgotten to build it. Tell me, what do you like in a home?"

"What do you mean? Where's your house?" James said.

"You know," Danghenam said, "if you had to design your dream home, what would it look like? I think you can tell a lot about a person by asking them about their dream home. They often build it in the way that their own minds are structured. For example, an engineer might describe a home with impeccably straight lines, every room boxed together, perfectly delineated and segregated. If you ask an artist they may describe a circular house built around a tree. Little things like that can tell you a lot about a person. So let me in a little, what would it be like?"

James brought his hand to his chin as tea was being poured. He had to look twice before he noticed that the kettle was pouring itself, Danghenam hadn't touched it. "Well, for starters it would have walls."

"Walls," Danghenam said. "Can do. Top notch idea. You're great at this, do you know that?" He picked up his cane and waved it around them, causing four bare walls, tan in color, to spring up around them, blocking out the trees. "How are these walls?"

"No, they need to be larger, and different material. How about stone? I've always liked the idea of stone walls."

"Stone walls, good. I like that. Sturdy, if a little cold. Stoic, too; stone walls build a good foundation to survive catastrophe well. So, let's see," Danghenam said, flicking the cane around. The walls changed into multicolored stone.

"How about a few windows?" James asked.

"I like it, desire to watch the outside world while remaining protected. Of course, the downside is that people can see in as well, although you can still hide things from windows." Danghenam complied with his request, putting a window wherever James pointed. He laughed. The magic of creation had put the last few hours at a comfortable distance behind him.

"And a few more levels, a staircase over there, some flowers in the corners, a stove there, a couch over there," James said, laughing with delight as the house grew and changed around him. The forest disappeared from view as the house formed around them.

"How do you like your new home?" Danghenam said.

James caught his breath and stopped laughing. The feeling inside him rapidly changed, soured. He struggled to keep a smile on his face. "It's a very nice house, but I don't think that it's my home. This is *your* home, I just helped you build it." In the silence that followed his admission he picked up his cup of tea and sipped at it. He made a delighted noise, the tea was sweet and warm, the flavor of honey exploding on his tongue.

Danghenam had a curious smile on his face as he watched James' every move. "You like the tea?" he asked. "Good, good. Now, let's talk about me and you." He placed his hands together in a steeple and sat back in his chair, his own cup untouched. "Now, I'm not sure that you're aware, but there's recently been a little hole that opened up inside of you."

"What are you talking about?" James asked. He set the tea cup down and shook his head. His vision blurred and he blinked hard. His thoughts were becoming muddled, and his tongue felt thick in his mouth. Everything started to feel distant and distorted. "What's going on, what's happening to me?"

"Do you feel that hole, that little tear in the fabric of your heart? I know you do, everyone does, though they don't always admit it when it happens." Danghenam began to pull at his gloves, taking them off finger by finger. "I'm going to give you something. Some regard it as a gift. Your father does, though he will never admit that to anyone, not even himself."

James began to sway on his seat. "I need to get back to my friends, something's wrong." He tried to stand but found that he couldn't; his arms and legs felt like they were made of lead. They wouldn't cooperate, and he didn't get more than an inch off his chair before collapsing back into it.

Danghenam pulled his glove all the way off. In the middle of his palm a starfish-shaped opening gaped and a creature slithered out, a snake-like thing with no eyes that snapped toward James. With Danghenam's other hand he took off his top hat, revealing little silver clasps set into his head. He unbuckled them and peeled off his face, the material stretching as it came off. James gasped. Underneath the fleshy mask, Gladhands smiled back at him. "I told you, I go by many names."

James struggled as hard as he could but he could not move a muscle. He sat, paralyzed, as Gladhands reached closer and closer to James' chest. The snake-like creature reached out toward the heat of his heart, hungry, elongating out from the starfish opening.

"Do you know why I wear this mask?" Gladhands asked as he placed his hand directly over James' heart. "Soon enough you will, you'll make a little mask for yourself, because it's easier that way."

A hollow pain bore into James' chest as the creature entered him. It was cold and wriggly as it wormed its way through the muscle and bone to dig into the little hole that had been torn in James' heart. It fit perfectly in the space, leaving a small frigid feeling right in the center of him. His vision doubled and everything got fuzzy, the sound of Gladhands growing distant as darkness crept in at the corners of his eyes. He fell heavily to the ground and lost consciousness.

CHAPTER SIXTEEN

James woke in a soft bed, sheets tucked in all around him so tight that he could barely move. The decor was feminine, pink frilled lace curtains ringed around the bed, pink comforter warming him. They weren't a vibrant color though; everything had a faded grey tinge to it. He stepped out of bed and discovered that his clothes had been stripped from him, leaving him in just his underwear.

He was in a stone room with a large vanity mirror sitting in the corner. He got dressed slowly, his head feeling dull and thick. As he belted his jeans on, the last few memories from before he blacked out came rushing back to him. He saw Gladhands' grinning visage leering over him, his hand reaching out, the thin, snake-like worm burrowing inside his chest. He rubbed the spot where it had entered. There was nothing there, not even a scar. Perhaps it had never happened.

A heavy oak door was the only entrance or exit to the room. He turned the knob and found it to be open. There was a hallway leading in two different directions, both lit by candlelight, a red carpet along the floor. It was cold, but not bone-chillingly so, more of an autumn chill. The kind that usually accompanies the rustle of dried leaves and a breeze across a bare neck.

Sounds floated down the hallway from one direction and he followed them, keeping his bare feet to the rug. There was an open door he peeked through. Jewel and Adlan were speaking together in hushed voices. They stopped when Jewel saw him peeking through the crack at the door.

"James, come in," she said. Her face was strained, there were wrinkles at the corners of her eyes. He stepped into the room. Chester was there as well, his arm angled up on a mantlepiece, his eyes locked on a roaring fire. Neither Chester nor Adlan turned to look at him when he entered. "How are you feeling?"

"Where are we?" James asked, his voice cracked and dry. "I was in someone's bed."

Adlan took a sip of a steaming mug that he held in his massive right hand. "Found you out in the woods, twitching on the ground. If you ask me, we should have left you there." The big man tossed the armor of Tantuk at his feet. "Found that near you. Not much use if you take it off."

James cognitively recognized that he should have felt some pain, some ache in his stomach at the dig from a friend, but something strange had blocked it. He felt it, but it was diminished, a shadow of what should have been. The room in the firelight looked strange as well, the previously bright colors of Jewel's dress and Adlan's armor, even of Chester's cloak, had all diminished. Like the curtains in the previous room, everything had a grey tinge to it. It was as though he were experiencing everything at a distance, or through a fogged up window. "Yes," he said quietly.

"What happened?" Jewel asked. "You ran off and we tried to follow, but your tracks just disappeared. We searched and searched, even camped out for a night. When we woke up, there you were, right where the tracks had stopped."

"I was gone for a day?" James asked. It didn't particularly surprise him. He didn't know whether it would be possible for him to be surprised, but he felt vaguely intrigued, the way someone would be about a slight change in the weather.

Adlan grunted, his eyebrows contracting as he looked at James for the first time since he entered the room. "What's wrong with you?" he asked. "Not that I would know, apparently I'm only a character, and that don't count for anything. Don't even have a father, according to you."

James sat down in front of the fire. The flickering flames and the heat of the embers didn't warm him. "I'm sorry if I hurt you guys. I was angry and frustrated, I should not have taken it out on you," he said, the words sounding hollow to his own ears. They had come to him so easily. Viewing the scene at a distance allowed him to know exactly what was right to say, even if there was no emotion behind the sentance.

The others must have felt differently, though, because Adlan's expression softened and Chester finally turned to him.

"It's all right, friend," Chester said, "we know that you didn't really mean those things." He placed a hand on James' shoulder and knelt down to his level. "I can't imagine what it's like, seeing these things happening to your dad and not knowing what you can do to help. But you should know that we're here for you. You don't have to bear that burden alone."

James put on a smile that he did not feel inside, his face was rubber and foreign. For something to do, he put out his hands to the fire and rubbed them together. "Where are we now?"

"We're in my castle," Jewel said. "When we found you we knew that we couldn't stay in a bad story for long, so we came here."

"Your castle?" James asked. "I thought you were from the story with the witch."

Jewel smiled at him. "I am in many stories, and this is one of them. We're safe here for the moment, and we can wait until you feel ready to travel again."

Chester cocked his eyebrow. "So what exactly happened back there?"

For the first time since Gladhands had placed his palm over James' heart, he felt an emotion strongly. That emotion, however, was the panic induced rush of anxiety. His heart began to race and his breathing came deeper, his eyes danced from Jewel to Chester to Adlan, all looking expectantly at him. They seemed a hundred feet tall, or perhaps he himself had shrunk down to the level of an ant. He felt a sudden certainty that they would desert him if they knew what had really happened, they would view him as tainted. And besides, he couldn't be sure what exactly had happened. For all he knew he tripped and hit his head on a rock. "I don't remember," he said, "I remember running into the woods and then everything went black. When I came to I was lying in the bed down the hall."

Adlan and Jewel nodded their heads with gentle smiles on their faces. Chester, on the other hand, looked at James intently with his one red eye. "You're sure you don't remember anything at all?" Chester asked.

James met Chester's stare with a blank one of his own. "I said I didn't." He turned to the others. "Let's keep moving toward Gladhands' story. There's no sense in wasting more time here."

Jewel nodded and they all gathered their things. James followed at a distance, his legs shaky and numb.

"The entrance is down here," Jewel said. They followed Jewel down the stone corridors of her castle to a room with a large reflecting pool sprawled across the ground. It looked like a floor of shimmering obsidian, there was nothing else in the room.

"What is this place for?" Adlan asked. "I've never felt such a somberness except for in a church. I don't think I like it."

Jewel smiled. "No, it is certainly not a happy room, though the story itself is a good one. My character makes her decision here to leave her family and defy her father to be with the man she loves." Her eyes locked on James briefly and then she looked away.

For some reason James liked the somberness of the room, the sorrow that the walls seemed to cry out with. It was a feeling that was not dulled nor fogged; he felt the sadness strongly. It was better than the blank feeling of isolation. "What do we do?"

"Just step out on it," Jewel said. "Let's do it together."

They all locked hands and stepped out onto the surface of the pool, the previous story falling away from them as they passed through the water.

CHAPTER SEVENTEEN

The ground came up to meet James hard and he stumbled, smacking his teeth against cobblestone and splitting his lip. The pain flashed and then dulled quickly as he put a hand to his face and it came away red. Gingerly he ran a tongue over his teeth, glad that they were all still there.

"Are you okay?" Adlan asked, pulling out his sheet of a handkerchief again and dabbing away at James' lip. "Did you not land on your feet properly?"

James pushed him away. The blood would dry soon enough, he didn't need to be coddled. He looked around. They were on a cobblestone bridge so tall they couldn't see either what they were suspended above or what the bridge was leading from or to. Mist shrouded them all around, the only thing James could see for sure was the bridge they were on. Eerily lit in the light of the moon, it was wide enough to travel comfortably, but at the edge there were no handrails, and looking down into the void below made him feel dizzy. "I'm fine," he said, though he could feel his lip beginning to swell.

But you're not fine, a voice whispered into his ear, *admit it, if only to yourself. You are not okay.*

James whipped around. "Who said that?" he asked, turning

this way and that. It had sounded like someone had been whispering straight into his ear. As far as he could see they were alone on the bridge. "Was that you, Chester?"

Chester was picking at the gap between his oversized front teeth. "What's that, James? You say something?"

"That voice, did any of you hear it?" James asked. A cold feeling emanated from the center of his heart. His eyes were wide and his shoulders hunched, every muscle in his body tense.

They gathered in a circle around James, concern evident on their faces. "No, we didn't hear a voice," Jewel said. "What did it say to you?"

They hadn't heard anything? Was he going crazy? He could have sworn that someone had spoken to him. Perhaps it was the story they were in. Then again, perhaps it wasn't. If something was truly wrong with him then his friends shouldn't know about it. They would think he was a freak, hearing voices where there were none to be heard. James set his face as straight as he could. He controlled it like a mask, each muscle relaxed, the skin rubbery.

*****

Now, I feel I must interject here for just a brief moment.

191

Hearing voices by itself is not an uncommon occurrence. I myself often have at least two or three arguing with one another. The normal person listens to all these competing things and chooses which sounds the most reasonable to them. HOWEVER, and I do have to emphasize that word, for those who have never experienced it, the first time hearing a foreign voice inside your head, one you have never heard before, it can be quite the traumatic thing. It throws you wildly off your game, and it is a true testament to James' character that he is able to roll with these punches as well as he is.

*****

"Nothing," James said, "it must have been the wind. Right, which way should we head, do any of you know this story?"

Lies, the voice said again. Adlan and Jewel began arguing back and forth about which direction they wanted to head in. Chester leaned over the side of the road, trying to peer down through the mist below them. *Lying to friends again, are we? Quite the habit we're making. Of course, it makes sense. Like father, like son,* the voice whispered. The cold, empty feeling that was inside James' chest began to grow larger, it was now a throbbing and dull ache. *They don't trust you, you know that, right? They all know what really happened to you, they know how you're broken inside, just like your father.*

Adlan and Jewel seemed to have decided which way to go. "You all ready?" Jewel asked James with a smile. James nodded and smiled back at her, feeling his cheek muscles open his mouth like a curtain. Jewel cocked her head to one side before reaching out a hand for his.

They walked hand in hand toward one end of the bridge, the mist flowing away from them as they neared it and covering where they had come from. The cobblestones under their feet were slick with moisture.

The bridge ended and a city unfolded before them, though this was no fantasy setting of medieval huts and castles. The buildings that sprawled around them had Gothic spires on the corners cutting up into the sky and gargoyles perched at the ledges, howling silently downward. The streets were cobblestone, like the bridge, and as they walked ahead a horse-drawn carriage clamored up from behind them and nearly ran them off the road.

"Thundering maniacs!" Adlan shouted after it with his fist raised. "We're walking here!"

As they watched, the carriage veered to the left and the right, teetering wildly. Finally it careened sharply to one side and slammed into one of the buildings, the reins to the horses snapping loose. The beasts ran off through the streets while the

193

carriage rolled and then slid to a stop in the middle of the street. The clattering of hoofbeats slowly receded.

"Was anyone driving that thing?" Chester said. "I didn't see anyone in the driver's seat, did you?"

Adlan shook his head. "If there were I'd have given them a mighty good thumping for it." They hurried over to where the carriage was sitting. Curiously, there was no one else in the street with them. With how loud the crash had been, James had expected the street to be packed immediately with curious onlookers, but instead nobody came out. He was sure, however, that he saw a few people looking out from behind drawn curtains.

"Quiet place, isn't it?" Chester said, giving voice to James' thoughts.

"Don't say, 'A little too quiet,' please for the love of the creator," Adlan said with a wry smile. "It's really just asking for trouble."

Chester grinned and nudged the large man in the ribs. Overly loud, he said, "A little too quiet, don't you think?" He ducked quickly to avoid the backhand that Adlan swung at him.

James was the first to explore the upturned carriage. "You were right," he said, "there's no one in the driver's seat." He peeked underneath, where the wood had splintered, the entire thing looking like a wounded animal. James touched a dark spot on the seat and grimaced when his fingers came up red and sticky.

Adlan knelt by the door of the carriage and leaned against it, straining with the effort. The frame of the carriage had warped, pinching the door in place. The windows were all darkened enough to where peering into them was pointless. With a grunt and a heave something gave way in the door and Adlan wrenched it off its hinges.

Chester stuck his head into the opening. "Does anyone have a candle or anything? I can't see a damn thing."

There were plenty of lit torches down the street; each house had one outside of its front door. Adlan jimmied one out of its holder and handed it to Chester.

The mouse stuck the torch in first and then ducked his head inside, almost immediately vaulting back out into the street, the skin under his fur paled to an ashy white. "Stay back!" he said, holding out his arm. "Ain't nothing good coming out of there."

A low rumbling growl came from inside the carriage. Chester and Adlan stood away, shielding Jewel with their bodies, but James crept forward, curiosity getting the better of him. A dull intrigue had caught him, and though consciously he knew that there should be some amount of fear in this situation, truthfully he felt very little at all.

From the darkness of the open door a pair of glowing red eyes emerged. An arm reached out and the eyes became something more. Crawling out from the carriage was something that appeared to be a man, although his features were horribly distorted. He had red, menacing eyes and sharp teeth that shone in the orange light of the flame. Though the nails on the tips of his fingers were trimmed like a human's, he held them curled like claws, and crawled along the ground like a beast.

Once free from the carriage the monster stood and fixed James with a stare. The monster's eyes were smouldering, but as James watched they seemed to have a swirling, distant fire burning within them. It was quite beautiful, that fire, and James had a fierce and sudden desire to be close to it, to wrap himself inside it and sleep long and well.

"Something smells warm," the monster said, his jaw going slack, his canines elongating. "You smell warm."

It would be wrong to say that James couldn't move in that situation. If he truly had to, he probably could have; however, he found that as the monster knelt beside him he didn't *want* to move. He *wanted* those lips upon his neck, to feel a pierce and then be filled with that wonderful, infectious fire.

The monster's mouth was open, his hot and wet tongue touching James' neck, and then he stopped. Sniffing mightily, his brow furrowed, the monster frowned at the child.

"Something's wrong, there's something tainted about you. You're no good."

The monster backed away from James, his lips curled in disgust. Turning away from them, his outline began to shimmer and waver as great wings sprouted out of his back. His body shrank and the wings pulled him up into the air as he turned into a bat. Within moments he was gone, flapping off into the night high above the buildings.

"What was that?" James asked. His previous desire seemed shameful, and his senses had returned.

Chester and Adlan moved forward, their faces pale. "That was the baron Vladimir Von Korloff," Chester said. "I should have known from the bridge which story we were in."

"You've been here before?" Jewel asked.

Chester nodded. "I had a late night with the daughter of a wealthy landowner here once, a woman named Ilsa. It scared me half to death when I woke up and the Baron was leaning over her. I hadn't known she was a big part of the story." His brow furrowed suddenly and he turned to James. "The Baron isn't one to pass up a meal, yet something about you soured him."

James took a step away from them. Their faces were dark as they looked down upon him, circling him. He gritted his teeth as a dull anger flared at the base of his stomach. What exactly were they implying?

It's because they hate you, the little voice whispered suddenly in his ear. Though surprised at hearing it again, James kept his face purposefully blank. He took another step backward. *They fear you. You're an outsider; you're not one of them. Why should they accept you?*

Adlan knelt and placed a hand on James' shoulder. His eyes were kind and his voice was soft when he spoke. "Do you know why he wouldn't touch you? Is there something we should know?"

Though he tried to keep his face perfectly still, his lip twitched into a sneer before he forced it back down. A tremor passed through him. *Listen to them,* the voice said, *they don't care that you're alive and well, they just care why that thing wouldn't touch you. A friend wouldn't say such things.*

James shrugged his shoulder from Adlan and stepped further away from the group. He held up his hands as though he could keep them at bay.

"James, what's wrong?" Jewel said. "You look angry. We're your friends, we're just trying to help. If there's something wrong we can help you."

They're not your friends, the voice continued, *you said it yourself, they're characters in a story. They don't really matter. And you know why that creature wouldn't touch you, don't*

198

you? It's because you're diseased; you're all black, rotting from the inside.

"I am not; you're a liar, there's nothing wrong with me," James said.

The others exchanged a glance that did not go unnoticed by James. "I think we should keep moving," Jewel said. "Chester, do you know where the next story is?"

The mouse sighed largely. "I do," Chester said, "but it's not the best place to go at night."

"Where is it?" Adlan asked.

Chester fixed them with a stare from his one good eye. "It's in the crypts."

CHAPTER EIGHTEEN

James felt their eyes on him the entire walk. He kept his face purposefully slack, smiling at all the appropriate times. It had become a tool to utilize; he noticed that the others paid less attention to him when he smiled and reacted as they expected him to react.

The streets were all deserted; their shoes rang on the cobblestone and echoed off the buildings. Torches burned brightly, lighting their way. Chester led them through the streets, regaling them with the story of how he and Ilsa had originally met.

"She was in the gardens in the story of Arterion. I was just passing through, having previously ended a clingy affair with the Princess D'angelo. She was a bit obsessed with me, but that's a story for another time. Ilsa was sitting in the gardens, her feet bare, surrounded by flowers. How was I to resist?" James recognized this as a cue to laugh, so he mimicked one as best he could. Chester seemed satisfied and continued his story. "I brought out my lute and strummed her a tune. She fell in love with me that moment, of course. We spent the day in the garden, but as night came on she said she had to return to her palace. She wanted me to come with her, and who was I to say no to a red-haired beauty such as herself?" He touched Adlan on the shoulder. "By the way, if you see anyone with red hair, let me know so I can duck down. Things didn't end well between us."

"No?" Jewel asked, a smile on her face. "I can't imagine why, was it all the other women you woo?"

Chester stuck his nose high up in the air. "You hurt my pride, madam. I only woo one woman at a time, a mouse has his standards. It's just that the women tend to change rather more quickly than they're okay with." He spread his arms wide. "What am I to say? My heart is a passionate and fickle thing."

They turned at a street corner and the buildings stopped abruptly. A large field of neatly manicured grass lay dotted with tombstones and surrounded by a wrought iron fence before them. The light from the moon cast an eerie glow over the entire thing, causing tree branches to look like skeletal fingers. A gate towered in the center of the fence, reaching high and arching over them.

"Ah," Chester said, "we're here. Might want to cover your ears, these things always creak in stories like this." The horrid squeal of rusting metal set his teeth on edge and made him wince.

They traveled over a small hill, stepping between the gravestones. James had heard it was seven years bad luck to step upon a filled grave, though that never quite made sense to him. A teacher had once told him that there were seven billion people alive in the world, an unfathomable number to his young ears. That same teacher had also told him that people had been people for over two-hundred thousand years. So it seemed to James that they couldn't *not* be stepping on someone's grave at all times. Even so, he inched around the headstones with the rest of them.

The mouse led them to a large mausoleum, a glowing white building with arched doors and a statue of an angel towering over them. It crested the top of a hill, and as they looked around, it very much seemed as though the entire graveyard was built around that one area.

"Are you guys ready?" Chester asked. "We'll have to go quietly. If it's night time hopefully the Baron is out hunting and we'll be able to slip in and be gone without him ever knowing that we were here."

Adlan pulled at the doors, his arms bulging with the effort. After a struggle they swung open, revealing a stairway down into the crypt. Spiderwebs clung to the sides of the opening and Jewel brushed them aside before entering. Chester drew his sword as they descended, as did Adlan.

In the light of the torch the crypt glowed a pale yellow; spiderwebs clung to everything except for a straight path in the dust at their feet. Along the walls were stacks of coffins with names etched into the bottoms. There were hundreds of them lining the hallway as they walked.

"This must be a whole family crypt," Adlan said, his voice echoing loudly off the stone walls.

The tracks in the dust led down the corridor; the hallways opened up into a large facsimile of a dining hall. There was a long table with people sitting all around, though no one moved as they entered. James crept forward, leaving the others behind, and approached the nearest seated person. When he came around the side of him he let out a noise of mild surprise. They weren't people at all, but statues dressed in real clothing. Dust even covered them. The entire room was designed like an everlasting feast was taking place. James signaled to the others that it was okay to enter.

At the far end of the room a coffin sat raised upon an elevated platform. "That's it," Chester said, pulling them forward. "That's the gate to the next story." They rushed forward and Chester tried to pry open the casket, but the top wouldn't budge. Even Adlan struggled against it to no avail, his arms straining and a bead of sweat on his forehead. "What's going on here?" Chester asked, kicking the coffin in frustration.

"It's locked," a hollow voice called out from behind them. They quickly turned; at the entrance to the room stood the same man that had menaced them outside of the carriage. He stood tall this time, his face noticeably less menacing, looking like less of a monster. He had a casual and bored air about him, his cheeks flushed red. His hair was parted to one side; he must have run a comb through it since the last time they had seen him. "I got rather tired of people popping in and out of it, though there's not much I can do if you come from the bridge entrance."

Chester stepped out and held his sword up menacingly. "Hello Baron, we meet again." His entire body trembled, everything except for the tip of his blade.

The Baron scowled. "Chester the Molester. I wondered if that was really you on the bridge or if my eyes were playing tricks on me."

"You guys know each other?" Jewel asked.

"You make it sound like a good thing," the Baron said. He pointed a finger at Chester. "I found this little rat in bed with my Ilsa."

"*Your* Ilsa?" Chester asked. "You're a vampire, you were sucking her dry."

The Baron drew himself up proudly, throwing his cloak over his shoulders. "She *invited* me in weeks before she got it in her head to go exploring and found you. In the story we make plans to go to the midnight theater that night. I wouldn't have been able to visit her if she hadn't. Honestly you make it sound like I was taking advantage of the poor thing. And here we had a nice date planned; I was going to take her out to a play and have a moonlit picnic after, and lo and behold, once I get into her room she's passed out next to this vermin. I check her over to make sure that she is all right, and he wakes up and starts slashing with that little sword of his, shouting that he'll save her from me. My story is a *love* story, you prick. Vampires can be in love too. Then, like a coward, he runs off, barely taking the time to button his pants before leaving."

Chester had begun to turn a light shade of red. "I had my pants fully secured, thank you very much. And tell me this, then. Why were you so menacing in the carriage?"

The Baron's mouth dropped open. "I had just been in an *accident*! How do you expect me to act? Here I am, all out of sorts, and someone kicks my door open and shoves a torch in my face. Of course I'm going to revert to my primal nature!"

"Accident, right," Chester chortled. "You're telling me you weren't responsible for that blood stain on the carriage seat?"

The vampire's mouth dropped open and his eyes gained a look of incredulity. "Are you kidding me? Why on earth would I kill my own driver *while I was being driven?* Do you think I enjoy pain or something?"

"Well, if some of the things Ilsa told me about you are true,"

Chester said.

The Baron paused as he caught sight of James. "You! I remember you. There was something strange about you."

James stepped away, suddenly feeling very exposed. Just as Adlan and Chester were putting their swords away, he drew his. "There's nothing strange about me at all, you're mad."

"James, what's wrong?" Jewel asked. "You can put your sword away, I don't think this man is a threat."

The Baron's nostrils dilated and he sniffed at the air. "It's the smell, there's something wrong with your smell. It's tainted, cold somehow." He walked forward, reaching out his arms. "Come here, let me smell you."

"There's nothing wrong with me!" James shouted and he turned to flee. The Baron's claw-like hands gripped the back of him and pulled him bodily off the ground. He felt a mouth pressed against his neck.

"No!" Adlan shouted and surged forward.

"We should kill him!" Chester shouted.

"Hold!" The Baron said with his teeth just above James' neck. "There's something in here, lodged in the heart. I think I can get it out, but only if you won't disturb me."

"You really think that we're going to just stand here while you suck him dry?" Chester asked, gripping his sword so tight that his paw turned white.

"Wait," Jewel said, a curious look in her eye. The look was soft and gentle, almost motherly in its concern. James didn't like it one bit. "There *has* been something that's gone wrong with you, hasn't there? You didn't want to admit it to anyone, didn't want to admit that you're having troubles."

James kicked hard against the Baron's shin as the anger flared up inside him again. They didn't really care about him, they just cared that he was broken; they couldn't have themselves *inconvenienced* with his troubles. The Baron dropped him with a gasp and he ran in the only direction left available to him, further into the crypts.

*****

A hallway opened off the main dining room downward, the dust and cobwebs growing thicker as he ran. His torch threw light a few feet in front of him, showing hallways branching off to the sides. It was a thick maze down there; he picked a hall at random and ducked down it into one of the first rooms he came to, leaning against one of the walls and catching his breath. The sound of footsteps echoed around him, but they were distant. His sudden departure had caught them all by surprise.

I told you they would never accept you, the voice said,

returning after being quiet for so long. James let his head fall into his hands. He really did not want to hear from anyone right now, let alone a disembodied voice.

"Go away," he moaned aloud.

"Go away?" a different voice answered. "But you came to me." This had come from outside his own head, he was sure of it. It was a high and lyrical thing, sounding like it belonged to a young girl.

James held the torch high, shining light into the room he was in. It was a long rectangular room, bare except for a protrusion down at the far end. The walls were made of stone, and though there was dust over the floor, there were no spider webs in there. He stepped gingerly toward the protrusion, close enough to see what it was.

A little stone circle, like a well no one bothered to finish, was built a foot off the ground. Lying next to it was a pile of rope. As James approached he saw that it was a wide hole that lowered down a good twenty feet into a pit. On the bottom, standing in a few feet of greasy black water, was the owner of the voice.

It was a little dark-haired girl dressed in a periwinkle blue dress. She smiled up at James, her eyes wide and innocent. "My hero," she said. She couldn't have been more than ten, and clasped her hands behind her back and swayed as she talked.

"You've come to save me. My prince charming."

"Why are you down in a well? How long have you been down there?" James asked.

She reached a hand up. Her fingers were long and thin. "Can you help me? I'm very hungry."

"How long have you been down there?" James repeated, gathering up the rope.

"Oh, far too long," she said, an eager look in her eye. James lowered the rope to her and she stretched her hand to it, her mouth opening wide in a grin.

Sitting himself down, James anchored himself against the edge of the well as she began to climb the rope. She was much heavier than he would have thought; he had to sweat and strain to hold on to his end. Finally, a hand thrust itself over the side, though it was not the hand of a child.

James recognized the thick fingers curled up over the side, the big forearms, the blue plaid shirt, the wedding band on the left finger. His father came out of the well and stood over him, though he was horribly deformed.

The eyes were milk white, the mouth gaping. He walked in shambles, not in the sure and confident steps that his father normally took. The smell, too, was off. Rather than the smell of his father's Old Spice, this thing smelled rotten, like a dead animal on the side of the road. Despite the pain of longing

James felt within himself he scuttled back. His father moaned and gnashed his teeth towards him.

"Dad?" James said in a quiet voice, his breath coming in gasps, a painful knot forming in his stomach. As the thing got closer James noticed something sticking out of his dad's left breast, a wriggling tail flailing wildly. It looked horrifyingly familiar.

"James!" a voice called out from behind him.

In that moment he knew; everything clicked together. Seeing it so plainly made it obvious; it was not that there was something wrong with his dad, it was that something was inside him burrowing away. James ignored the call from behind him and lunged forward into the arms of his father. His hands found the wriggling tail and grasped at it, even as his father fell on him. With the hot smell of rancid decay all around him and his father's teeth snapping toward his face, James tugged at the tail.

Strong fingers encircled James' neck and squeezed, crushing his throat in a powerful grip, but still he would not let go. Things went black for James as he heaved at the wriggling tail, wrenching it out of his father's chest. As it finally broke free, the lack of oxygen shut him down and he lost consciousness.

CHAPTER NINETEEN

A light slapping on his cheek woke James. There was a pounding, pulsating pain behind his eyes. His friends were all around him, staring down at him. Even the Baron was there, his pale features scrunched in concern.

"What happened? Is my dad all right?" James asked.

"That wasn't your dad," the Baron answered, "that was the Illudere. It plays a part in my story."

James stood and looked over the edge of the well. The little girl was back down there, smiling up at him. A shiver ran down his spine and he quickly got away from the hole. "So that wasn't my father?"

The Baron shook his head. "No, it reflects the greatest fear of the person it is hunting. Can I ask you a question James?"

James nodded. A sudden exhaustion had taken him; his limbs felt heavy and weak.

"Why was there a cavum worm in the illusion of your father? How do you know about them?"

James looked to his other friends. Adlan and Chester were both seated cross-legged next to him; the big man had a hand to his shoulder. Jewel was behind him, cradling his head in her lap. A sudden wave of shame and guilt grew inside him. He knew how horrible he had been to them, and yet here they were beside him, helping him. He didn't deserve to have friends like this; he deserved to be abandoned, left in a field to rot. Hot tears of shame sprang to his eyes. "I think I have one in me," he said. The dam burst, and everything that he should have told them before came rushing out. He told them of what really happened after his meeting with Danghenam, and how he took off his mask and revealed himself to be Gladhands. "I should have realized," he said.

Jewel hugged him closely from behind, and he allowed himself to be comforted. "That's how he works, he wears masks and tricks people into believing either that he's not there or that he's something harmless. You shouldn't feel bad."

"He put one of those worms in me," James said in a quiet voice.

Jewel turned to the Baron. "What do you know about these things?"

The Baron stroked at his chin, peering inquisitively at James. "I occasionally travel out from this story; the elves from some of the fantasy stories are quite a delicacy, their blood is almost fruity, with a full-bodied nose."

Adlan cleared his throat loudly. "We're talking about the worms, not your favorite meals."

"Yes," the Baron said and shook his head. "I've come across

them in a few stories. Cavum worms, as they are called, grow deep underground. They feed on sadness, nestling right into the heart of the victim. Tell me, James, have you been hearing a voice talking to you?"

James put his head down, his cheeks burning with shame. "Yes."

"The voice is the worm's most powerful tool. It undermines the host, feeding off worry, fear, and despair. As it eats a larger and larger hole the voice grows stronger, until the entire host is nothing more than a shell of negative emotions."

"Can we get it out?" Adlan asked, his eyes big with worry. "James was able to with the shambling thing. Can we do the same?"

"I can get it to show itself, but James has to be the one to pull it out," the Baron said.

Chester, having listened to the entire thing in silence, suddenly spoke up. "I wouldn't trust him," he said, his arms across his chest. His one eye was narrowed in suspicion. "That's not a man, it's a vampire, lest you forget."

"And you're a mouse," the Baron said, straightening himself. The two of them looked very much like stags out in the wild ready to butt heads. "I shouldn't have to deal with this type of prejudice. You're the one who slept with Ilsa, I would remind you of that."

Jewel placed a hand upon Chester's shoulder. "He *has* heard of them before. We should at least listen to what he has to say."

Chester stomped his foot and shrugged off Jewel's hand. "Fine, trust the bloodsucker. Disregard my opinion entirely." He stepped forward and stuck a finger in the Baron's face. "Know this, I'll be standing right here with my sword if you try anything foul."

The Baron smiled and brushed him away like a fly. "Are you ready for this? First take off that chest plate; it's where the worm will come out," he said. James nodded and shrugged off the armor. "Okay, I'm going to start sucking your blood. I'll only drain a little, but it should be enough to get the worm thinking that the host is being threatened. Self-preservation is a strong instinct in them; it should show itself, giving you enough time to grab hold of it."

Chester drew his sword. "I'm watching you."

James nodded. He was tired of feeling this way, tired of the colors being muted, tired of being suspicious and paranoid about friends, tired of feeling broken.

The Baron latched onto his neck, fangs sliding through his skin easily. Though the fangs were long and sharp, it didn't feel like more than two little pinpricks. James heard a rushing sound in his ears that throbbed louder and louder. The sensation was altogether very pleasant, almost euphoric, until

214

the burning feeling in his heart began. He gasped with pain; something was digging straight up and out, tunneling through his skin.

"There it is," Jewel said.

With trepidation, James looked down. Just like he had seen with the apparition of his father, a green, worm-like thing with sharp little teeth was hanging out of a hole in his chest. This one was larger though, having had time to feed, and colored black. It hissed toward the Baron.

"Now, James, grab it!" Adlan shouted, his voice jolting James to action.

His hand shot up and grabbed the slimy thing by its middle. It squirmed against him, wrapping around his hand and biting into him several times. With a Herculean effort James gathered all his strength and tore the thing out of his chest; he sighed as he felt the slimy blockage leave his heart. The Baron released James and grabbed at the cavum worm, throwing it down the open well.

With the cavum worm gone, James did not experience the return to normalcy that he expected. Rather the opposite, actually. Things began to fade, his vision going white. He felt empty inside. The world fell away from him in a dizzying haze.

"We have to find something to put in there," the Baron said from a distance. "It was larger than I anticipated."

Jewel stepped forward. "Leave this to me," she said as she pushed everyone away from James. He registered her only as a faint pink blurriness hovering over him, the cloud of white too strong. It felt like he was trapped within a cotton ball, everything muted.

A pressure built in his chest and he felt himself pulled back to reality. The scene around him materialized, the colors vibrant once again. The hollow emptiness was gone from inside him. "What was that?" James asked, sitting up. "What did you put in me?"

Jewel smiled. Her face was drawn and pale, her hands shaking, but she looked happy. "Like I told you, a woman has to have some secrets," she said.

*****

As strange as it may be, feeling all of your emotions once more does have its downsides. You see, you can't pick and choose which ones you get to feel, and with the numbness and despair gone from James, the memories of how he had been acting brought about an undesirable emotion. Shame. It was stronger than before, undiluted. He felt the raw emotional hurt that went along with his behavior.

He knew that the cavum worm had been a partial reason for

him to act poorly toward his friends, but he also knew that he had started doing that before the worm ever entered his body. He had been cruel to them before even running off in the woods, and his face burned with the thought.

"Guys," he said, stopping them as they walked back up to the statue dining hall, "I have to say something." The others turned around and faced him. "I'm sorry if I've been acting like a jerk. There's no excuse for treating your friends poorly, and you are all my friends."

Adlan placed a huge hand on his shoulder, almost knocking him down. "I forgive you, but I also reserve the right to call you out on it if you act like a brat again."

Chester and Jewel smiled at him as the Baron walked up. "I forgive you as well," the Baron said.

"What did he ever do to you?" Chester asked.

The Baron shrugged. "I don't ever get anyone apologizing to me. I thought it might be a nice thing to experience."

James laughed. "Baron, do you know what the next story is? The one that you have chained up so tightly?"

The Baron suddenly grew somber, standing tall. His face fell and his eyes darkened. "It is a nightmare realm of unimaginable horrors. I would not go there if I were you. Turn back and save yourself the insanity."

Everyone gathered around him. James felt the first tinglings

217

of fear in the pit of his stomach. "We have to go through it, unless any of you know a different way to get to Gladhands' story. Do any stories have multiple ways to them?"

Jewel nodded. She still looked very pale, and she coughed into a pink handkerchief before saying anything. "There are some, but not any close by. What is so bad about this next story?"

The Baron took a deep breath. With the gravity of a deathbed confession, he spoke. "Gnomes," he said.

Startled, the rest of the group laughed. "Gnomes?" James asked. "Like those little statues that people put in their gardens? We had those once, but they kept getting stolen from our lawn."

The Baron put his head in his hands, his face drawn downward in a fierce grimace. "Why does everyone laugh at me when I tell them that?"

"Maybe it's because you're afraid of something shin high and harmless," Chester said.

"They're not harmless!" the Baron shouted. "They're terrible little creatures and everyone thinks that they're so great, that they're just wonderful little cherubs, but they're not."

Jewel had a hand over her mouth, trying to stifle her own laughter. "What's so bad about the gnomes?"

The Baron crossed his arms. "They spread like vermin underground, digging everywhere, thinking that they have the right to everything underground. I chained up the gate because they kept coming here and digging in the lower crypts, disturbing my ancestors, and if you try to reason with them like a rational being they just start biting your ankles. They swarm you."

"You're a vampire, why didn't you bite them back?" Adlan asked.

The Baron scoffed. "As if I would lower myself to feasting on their blood. They smell bad enough, I can't even imagine what they taste like."

"Well," James said, "can you at least unlock the gate so we can get through?"

The Baron stared around at the lot of them, tapping his fingers against his arm, a look of frustration on his face. "I'm going with you. You are all underestimating these little devils, I can see it in your eyes."

"As if we want your help," Chester said, spitting on the ground.

"Not only would I be a great asset to your group," the Baron said, "but also you have little choice. I won't unlock the gate unless you let me come with you."

James looked between them all. Chester was shaking his head back and forth slowly. "All right, let's go then. No sense in wasting more time here."

The Baron unlocked the coffin and it swung open, revealing a red plush velvet-lined interior. "Going for stereotypical?" Chester asked as he put one foot up into the coffin. "Because you've nailed it right on the head."

"He really is an unpleasant little rodent, isn't he?" The Baron said to James. "Why do you keep him around?"

James shrugged and followed Chester through the coffin into the next story. The light from the torches fell away as he tumbled through. He fell hard on the ground, disoriented. It was completely dark. A scraping sound came from off in the distance. He couldn't even see his hand in front of his face. A sudden pain jarred his shoulder and he was knocked over again.

"Did I just kick someone?" Adlan's voice called out. "I can't see a damn thing."

James rubbed his head. "That was me, I can't see anything either."

A sudden light flared up as the Baron popped into view holding a lit torch. They were in a dirt tunnel that led down, twisting in on itself. Jewel came last, falling through the ceiling and landing hard on the ground.

"Are you okay?" James asked, helping her up.

She nodded and began to cough. The sound was loud and wet, echoing down the hall.

The Baron quickly put a handkerchief to her mouth, stifling

the sound. "You want to be careful here. The little ankle biters will swarm you." He signaled for the others to follow him down the tunnel.

"Have you been here?" Adlan asked, crouching low so as not to scrape his head on the ceiling.

The Baron nodded gravely. "Though the rat there may think I am an uncivilized beast, I do have proper respect for law and order. When the gnomes originally began coming into my story and digging in my crypts I thought to reason with their ruler, thinking that I would be able to present my case respectfully and he would comply."

"Well, what happened?" James asked.

The Baron snarled. "Beasts like these apparently don't have a king, or a republic, or anything of the sort. They simply do things by hive-mind. They saw me coming and just grabbed me and kept me hostage in a pit. They, of course, didn't realize my particular power of transfiguration, so as soon as they were asleep I was able to fly out of there, but I tell you I was mightily offended!"

"I bet you were, having to spend half of a night getting dirt on your fancy cape there," Chester said.

The Baron pulled at Chester's shoulder and looked him in the eye. His fangs were bared and his eyes turned a bloody red. "Some day soon, rat, you and I are going to have a little conversation and settle our differences."

"I welcome it!" Chester said. "Let's settle it right here and now."

Another spasm of coughing racked Jewel's body and she doubled over. Her entire being seemed to contract, trying to purge whatever was ailing her out of her body. Adlan rubbed her gently on the back, pulling out his handkerchief. "Are you all right, there, missy?"

Jewel nodded. When she gave Adlan the handkerchief back it was spotted with blood.

"What's wrong with you?" James asked, putting his hand on her shoulder. Her skin felt feverishly hot and was soaked in sweat, even though she was shivering.

"I think it's just a cold," Jewel said when she could catch her breath, "I wouldn't worry about it." She stood straight and took a few deep breaths. "I'm okay," she said after a moment. "Where to?"

As the group moved away Adlan pulled James back and knelt down next to him. "I'm worried about Jewel," he said in a hushed voice, his brow furrowed. "It ain't normal for characters to get sick like this. Something's happened to her."

James nodded. "Do you think it has to do with whatever she did to me?"

Adlan frowned. "I don't know. If it does, then it was her

choice, and you shouldn't feel bad about it. But I don't know that it was that." He looked back to make sure that the others were far out of listening range and bent in even closer. "There's always been a lot of rumors about Jewel there. Strange rumors. She's known throughout more than a few stories. Now, that may not mean anything to you, but let me put it in perspective. I am the greatest warrior in my story. No offense to you, but your little baby self doesn't count. But even I am not known outside of a small circle of warriors that get together for a pint of honey beer every now and again. But Jewel there, she's known in just about every story she goes into. There's something special about that one, and the fact that she's getting sick has got me more than a bit concerned."

James nodded. He was beginning to grasp the severity of the situation. "Well, what can we do?"

Adlan shook his head, his braided beard swinging back and forth along his chest. "I have a little pet theory that her health is tied in some way to the strength of Gladhands. He's getting stronger; there's no doubt in my mind anymore about that, and I think we're getting closer to his story."

"Are we?" James asked. "I can't keep track of it at all. It just feels like we're jumping story to story."

Adlan shrugged. "Technically we are. But the stories should be getting darker and darker as we get closer to his. It's not a fixed plane, but it's not exactly fluid either."

James had a thought and his face fell. "Adlan, how do we beat him?"

"Gladhands?" Adlan said, "I don't know." There was a moment of silence and then Adlan shook James on the shoulder, smiling warmly. "But what I do know is that with both you and Jewel on the same side, he doesn't stand a chance."

The unwavering confidence of the giant did little to make James feel better. Jewel might stand a chance against Gladhands, but the last time he had come into contact with the monster he hadn't even *recognized* him. How could he fight something like that? "Yeah, I guess so," he said and they rejoined the party.

Jewel had regained some of her color when they got back, though the Baron and Chester were still glaring daggers at one another. "So," James said, "which way do we go?"

"The only way there is to go," the Baron said, "down." He led them down the tunnel, holding the torch aloft. The slope gradually declined to a point where they had to step sideways to keep their footing, holding on to one another as they descended. The path wound around on itself, spiraling down in a corkscrew fashion. Near the end, where the slope seemed to be leveling out, the Baron held up his hand to stop them all.

"I thought you said this was a gnome city," James said.

"Where are they all?"

"Yeah, by the amount of quaking you did in your shoes I would have thought they were swarming the place," Chester said.

The Baron scowled. "Just because you lot are blind doesn't mean that your surroundings don't exist. Can you not see the tunnels in the walls? The little noses peeking out that disappear as soon as you turn your head? We're surrounded, and we have been ever since we first got in here."

"If there's so many of them, why do they hide? Numbers matter a lot in a battle, and I'd fight a single lion over a hundred lynxes any day," Adlan said.

"They're all terrified of the sphinx," the Baron said in an offhand manner.

"Sphinx?" Jewel asked, coughing on the back of her hand. "What sphinx? Vladimir, do you know the name of it? There's not too many of them."

The Baron scratched at his chin. "I did once. It's something sinister and snakelike. Sisyphus, or Secretariat," he said, muttering to himself.

"Slytherax?" Jewel asked as her eyes widened.

The Baron smiled, snapping his fingers. "Slytherax! That's it. But don't worry, we won't have to go anywhere near him. At the bottom of this pit there's an intersection where you can enter several different stories. I'll lead you there, and from there you can travel wherever you want, but I'll have to return to my story."

"All the better for it," Chester said, his arms crossed.

A new fit of coughing doubled Jewel over and she placed a hand on Adlan's shoulder to stay steady. "No," she said when she caught her breath. "The sphinx, that's where we need to go."

"Why?" Chester asked. "How could that possibly benefit us?"

Jewel took a few deep breaths and straightened herself out, avoiding the curious looks the group gave her. "Because it's guarding the Arbiter, or so I've heard."

"The sword?" Adlan asked. "Like I said, I've got a sword right here, James has a sword, Chester has a sword. We don't need any more weapons, we've got enough."

Jewel shook her head. "No, Gladhands won't be affected by any of your normal weapons, he's too strong for that. I think the Arbiter is the only thing that will help us defeat him once and for all. We have to get it."

"Do you know anything about this story?" Chester asked.

"I didn't realize we had gotten so close to it. I've never been in it myself, but I know somewhat about it. Only one person can enter the lair of the sphinx, and there they are tested."

"How are they tested?" James asked.

"I don't know," Jewel said, "but if you slay the sphinx then

226

the sword is yours. Once you have the sword we have a chance at defeating Gladhands." She paused, biting at her lip. "It's a Jamie story."

CHAPTER TWENTY

As they walked lower and lower in the cavern James could feel thousands of eyes watching him. The gnomes were growing braver, unabashed in their curiosity about this newcomer. The Baron swatted at the holes they stuck their ugly little faces out of.

"I wish I could kill them all," the Baron said, swatting his hand at a particularly brazen one. "Believe me when I say I'm waiting on the creator to make a new story so I don't have to be next to these little ankle-biters."

They came upon a wide open section of the cavern with a ledge that wound down to the depths. Across the way a dark archway sat, and the Baron pointed one of his gnarly fingers toward it. "There," he said. "That's the sphinx's lair, though I'll say it again, I can just take you to the next story."

Jewel stumbled, catching hold of Adlan's shoulder before falling. "You all right there, missy?" he asked.

"Just a bit light-headed," Jewel said, though her eyes were half way shut and her face pale and clammy.

Adlan grabbed hold of her shoulders and slung her over his back, carrying her as one might a backpack.

At the entrance to the archway James steeled himself, a light sheen of sweat coating his brow. "Why do I have to be the only one?" he asked.

"That's how it is in the story," Jewel said. "But if Jamie can do it, so can you."

"I'm beginning to see why you hate that little guy so much," James said to Adlan.

The tunnel through was dark and rimmed with cobwebs, and it seemed as though a deep heat emanated from where he was headed. The archway opened up to a small room with a simple pedestal in the middle, an ornate old sword laid across it.

The weapon had a jagged, bloody blade and wicked looking spikes along the hilt. There was a black crusty substance that had dried on the blade, and the thing seemed to emanate cold, even in the warmth of the room. When he picked it up his entire hand felt empty, almost as though the cavum worm were inside him again. Though he detested the feeling, he gripped the sword tightly.

Underneath where the sword had lain words were etched into the pedestal. "There is a creature of unfathomable evil in the next room. Do not speak to it, nor listen to its lies. It is a monstrous thing. Stab this sword through its breast at the first opportunity you get and the sphinx will die forever."

James frowned, but held the sword tighter as he walked

through the archway on the other side. His palms were sweating, and it seemed as though his body had forgotten how to breathe. In and out, he had to remind himself. In and out.

At the end of that tunnel the room opened up into a gigantic hall. At the far end, breathing in slow breaths that pushed his hair to the side, the sphinx slumbered. It was a majestic thing, with pure onyx feathers shimmering all along its body in every place except for a small patch right next to its heart. It had the body of a lion with the wings of a bird, and its head, though vaguely serpentine, was also disturbingly human. The thing was terrifying, that much was true, but there was also a sort of wondrous beauty about it. He found himself wondering what it would look like up in the sky, blotting out the moon with its tremendous wings. There wasn't much room to fly in that cavern, and despite his fear, James felt a little sorry for the creature.

Still, he swallowed down any pity he felt and crept forward, the sword held aloft, until he was standing right before its breast, inches from the only place he could plunge the blade in.

He hesitated. It all seemed wrong, it didn't seem like something that his father would write. This was senseless slaughter, a killing of a beautiful creature solely because a rock said to. The tip of his sword wavered and he tried to force himself to remember that this was a fictional animal, it wasn't *really* real. But then again, if this sphinx wasn't real, then his friends out in the hallway weren't real either, and hadn't he already learned that lesson?

His father, he had to think of his father. Of how he sat in that chair with the amber liquid loosely held by his fingertips, of the glass falling and shattering, of the milky white eyes that saw nothing but snow. With one last attempt at resolve he brought the sword up and tensed his shoulder, ready to throw his entire body weight behind it.

He took a step back and the resolve left his body in a woosh of air. Fictional or no, he couldn't kill this thing in cold blood. He let the sword slip from his fingers and the metal rattled on the stone floor. He was thankful not to be touching the blade anymore, not to be feeling that frigidness.

The sphinx opened its eyes immediately. "So, are you here to kill me, then? I'll not make it easy for you." It emphasized each "S" with a slithering of its serpentine tongue, but the eyes were human, colored a deep green with flecks of gold.

James took a step back. He had not expected such an eloquence from the creature, no matter how majestic. "You can talk?"

"As can you," Slytherax said with a wry smile. "Pray use that ability to answer my question, are you here to kill me?"

"I was going to, I guess," James said. "I think I'm supposed to, according to the stone out there. But it seems wrong. Sure, you're big, and you're threatening."

It was such an odd thing to see, but it looked to James like the sphinx *smiled* at that, standing a little taller and looking mighty pleased. "Yes, I'm quite terrifying, aren't I?"

"Oh yes," James said. "Your claws look sharp."

"Sharp as razors," Slytherax said, holding them aloft. They looked like the talons of an enormous eagle. "Could cut through metal like butter, built for tearing my enemies asunder."

"The thing is, you don't seem like a threat to me. I mean, what harm are you doing? You're just sitting here, and I need a sword that you are guarding. There's nothing inherently bad about sphinxes."

"Actually some of us are quite lovely," Slytherax interjected.

"So no," James said, resolute. "I don't think I'm going to kill you."

Slytherax smiled again, his gigantic form shimmering and shrinking down. In a few moments time, where a monumental mythical creature had been, there stood a simple gnome, shorter even than James. The only hint that he was larger than life were his eyes; they were still vibrant green and seemed to pulse with a strange sort of otherworldly energy. "Glad to hear it. My name is Tinker," he said, sticking out a hand.

"I thought your name was Slytherax?" James asked, shaking the small creature's hard little hand.

The gnome waved the notion away. "That's just what I call myself when I'm in my sphinx form. It's much more terrifying than 'Tinker the Sphinx' isn't it?"

James was forced to nod in agreement.

"Now, you'll be wanting that sword, I'm guessing. You seem to have gotten a bit older than the last time, but only Jamie would know not to kill the sphinx." The gnome turned around and gestured toward where he, as a sphinx, had stood. In his place was a small stone pedastel, like the one in the hallway outside but shining with a radiant blue light and with the sword stuck straight out the top of it. "Go ahead," Tinker urged.

With a hand that shook more than he would have liked, James grabbed hold of the sword. As soon as he touched the pommel a wonderful feeling of warmth spread through him, like the sun was shining directly on his face. It wasn't like he felt giddily happy, but more that he felt sure and confident with himself, like he could handle problems as they came.

The blade felt light within his hands, and swung easily. Tinker drew out James' old sword and tossed it aside. "You won't be needing that."

"Thank you," James said. It seemed like such a simple thing to say for what he had been given, but he hoped the amount of emotion that went into it would be recieved.

Tinker just nodded and waved to him. "You should be getting back to your friends now, they'll be getting worried."

*****

"Did you get it?" Adlan asked as James walked out.

He nodded and pulled out the glistening blue blade. It seemed to hum with its own energy, vibrating within his hands and casting a pale blue light everywhere.

"It makes me feel warm just looking at it," Adlan said.

"Jewel, how are you feeling?" James asked.

She smiled at him, though she held a hand up against the wall to steady herself. "Much better, James, thanks."

The Baron put up a hand and backed away from the blade. "Can you put that away? Something about the light hurts me."

"It's because you're evil," Chester said with a sneer. "James should drive it through your black heart."

"It's not because I'm evil," the Baron protested.

Jewel coughed into her hand and held up a finger. "Actually, it is because you're evil, unfortunately. You're not *terribly* evil, so it doesn't agonize you to be in its presence. But you are slightly evil, being a vampire."

"Not all vampires are evil!" the Baron said.

234

"Yeah but you're sort of bad," Jewel said before putting her hands up. "I'm not judging, and I don't think anyone in this party is."

"I am," Chester said.

"I'm just trying to tell you why the blade hurts you to look at. It's the Arbiter," Jewel said.

"And what about the Arbiter makes it so unpleasant to be in the presence of?" the Baron hissed. James slid the sword into his old case and the vampire seemed to calm down a little.

"It gives strength to good characters and is proportionally damaging to evil creatures," Jewel said.

"Well isn't that just bloody wonderful," the Baron said, sneering.

Chester pushed past the Baron and down the walkway. "Serves you right for being evil. Notice I don't get affected by it at all." The mouse led the way with the Baron sulking in the back.

"Why is there such tension between you two?" James asked.

The Baron stroked at his fine chin and watched as the mouse slunk away into the distance. "I know why I have a disliking of him. I caught him trying to be fresh with my maiden, but as to why he dislikes me so much, I can only speculate. I think he may be one of those men who needs to have every woman in the room fall in love with him or his ego is bruised. They're a very delicate breed. He probably took Ilsa's invitation to mean something rather more than it really did."

The hallway they were traveling in opened up into a huge underground pit with a pathway circling lower around the edge. The center was hundreds of feet down, and James felt his stomach perform several flips inside him when he peered over the edge. Thankfully the walkway was wide enough that he could stay close to the wall and avoid looking down.

"Is this where we're supposed to be going?" James asked, keeping hold of the wall at all times. Why hadn't they done the sensible thing and put a guard rail in?

The Baron nodded. "Yes, at the bottom of this pit there is an intersection between several stories, and I believe that you'll be able to travel wherever you want from there."

James nodded, bit his lip, and kept walking.

As the walkway wound down toward the dark nadir of the cave a curious thing began to happen. Far above them, drifting down lazily on the air currents, little sparkles of white began to flutter. The temperature in the cave went from a balmy humidity to a goosebump-prickling frigidity within a few minutes, and James rubbed at his arms. His breath came out in a fog before him. "Is that snow?" James asked as the white powder fell down around them. "Is it snowing in here?"

Jewel, already looking sick and pale, began another coughing fit. This one was louder and longer than her previous ones, echoing in the cavern, and Adlan placed a hand on Jewel and held her close. "Jewel, is everything all right?"

When she regained control of herself Jewel had a crazed, manic look in her eyes. "I don't like snow. I don't like it one bit."

The powder dusted the walkway, making it slippery and treacherous. James found himself taking great care with every step, making the traveling slow but sure. As they wound down carefully they finally were able to see the bottom. It was a circular floor with several arches on all sides of the place. On the floor a few inches of snow had built up around their ankles, the cold seeping down the sides of James' shoes.

"Which way do we go?" James asked. "Which way to Gladhands?"

Jewel coughed again mightily, her arms shivering in the snow. Adlan picked her up and cradled her against his breast as easily as one might a child. "I don't know, lad, but wherever we go we should do it fast. Jewel's not getting any better."

She placed a trembling hand upon his chest. "Adlan, the only thing that will help is when we beat Gladhands. We have to keep going."

Standing in the middle, James felt an overwhelming sense of frustration. There was no clear path. In all the others someone had known which way to go, but even thinking upon that he knew it was possible they were just wandering about in circles. There was no set way, and it frustrated him and angered him. If only there was a way to just change things, to bring Gladhands there so they could finish it once and for all. He closed his eyes, his hands balled up into fists, his heart beating rapidly. As he thought harder and harder the blood rushed in his ears, creating a sound like the ocean. There had to be a way to bring him. He concentrated on what he remembered of the creature's face. That mask that clasped onto the sides of his head, the moldy suit that he wore with worms peeking out of the pockets, the white gloves covering thin and skeletal fingers. He could picture the monster so clearly, it was like he was there. Someone gasped.

"Oh, hello," a silky voice called out.

CHAPTER TWENTY-ONE

Startled, James opened his eyes. The snow fell heavier, but standing in one of the archways was the masked man he sought.

Gladhands stood with a languid sort of boredom, his back leaning against the wall. His eyes, the shimmering multifaceted eyes that burned with such a strange heat, bore into James with an intensity that his body language didn't match. "You're here," James said in a disbelieving voice.

"I'm just about as surprised as you are about that. I was having a wonderful snack over in one of the children's stories and suddenly," he made a theatrical flourish with one hand, "here I am. I see my little gift wasn't appreciated. I should have known that you weren't really in a well one story over."

Adlan made like he was going to rush forward but as soon as he let go of Jewel she dropped to the floor and he had to stop. Chester had his sword pulled, and the Baron was watching curiously, but James held his hands out to keep them back. This was his fight. Fingering the handle on the Arbiter, he began to feel steady on his legs. The sword gave him strength. The fear in front of him was tangible, something to be dealt with. "Gift?" James said, "I fail to see how a worm burrowing inside of me is a good thing. Or is that how you see it? Do you see yourself as the hero here? You're not, you're evil."

Gladhands' form was so thin, it wavered as he took a step toward James. "That's not how I see it at all. I'm simply going to say that when you talk of good and evil in absolutes, you're doing a disservice, you're simplifying things down to black and white." The monster took another step toward him, breathing the smell of hot sewage out in a wave. "What I'm saying is that my gift to you, and to your father, makes these insipid little tales more *interesting*. If you have to be confined to the two dimensions of a page, wouldn't you want to at least be engaged by it? There is no such thing as a life without unhappiness; you're delusional if you think so. If all you had was happiness, it would all seem flat to you."

"But you're taking over all the stories! You're changing them, making them dark and scary and wrong!" James cried out. "You need to go back to your original story. That's your place."

Gladhands clenched his gloved hand into a fist. "My place?!" His voice was thunderous and shook the cavern as he bellowed. As he raged the light in the room seemed to dim, and the cold intensified. "You do not have even the slightest conception of what I am, and you try to tell me my place? I am a part of every story the creator has made because *I am a part of him.*" He took a step toward James, his hands petting at the scowling face he wore. "These masks may change but it's me, it's always me." His voice lowered and his eyes softened. A note of infinite sadness entered his voice. "Can you even imagine being created just to be hated? To know deep within yourself that without your ugliness there could be no beauty? Without your horror there could be no love? And yet, despite the deeply important part I play, I am despised."

The comment confused James. This was most definitely Gladhands, his mask bolted onto the sides of his head, the long slender black-and-white suit, but something was very different. Perhaps he was just seeing a new side of him, or, he thought and his resolve hardened, a new mask. "You are a liar, and you are destroying my dad. You have to go back to your story, back to your place."

Gladhands' face fell, his eyes drooped at the sides and his mouth was soft with a slight downturn at the corners. "Very well. I'll play the part of your villain. It's all I've ever been."

James tugged out the Arbiter and brandished it before him. The sword gave off a fierce blue light; Gladhands squinted at it but did not back away.

"Where did you get that neat little thing?" he asked.

"It will be your downfall," James said.

Gladhands sighed, pulling his white gloves off. "I had hoped that you would be different, that giving you my gift would allow you to see things from my perspective. I guess I was wrong." With his gloves off, two cavum worms crawled out of his palm and onto the ground. Larger than the one he had previously planted in James, these worms shook the ground when they fell, taking up a large part of the cave floor. James stood before them, his sword drawn, and Adlan, Chester, and the Baron joined him.

"Jewel?" James asked.

"I've got her propped up against the wall, but I don't think that she'll be much good in this fight," Adlan replied.

As the worms hissed and snapped at the warriors, Gladhands reached up and unbuckled the clasps on the side of his face, pulling his white mask off. James gasped. What was underneath was pure horror.

His face was composed of worms and maggots crawling around each other, shining with moisture, though they kept the general form of a face. The mouth was a gaping black hole with rotted teeth and a thick purple tongue that hung out the side. There were no eyes, those had come off with the mask, just fleshy bits of skin and maggots and worms. "Can you see me?" Gladhands asked. "Look at what your father created; I am the villain, I am always the villain. I will always be the villain."

James swallowed hard and grasped onto his sword tightly as Gladhands advanced.

Gladhands pulled maggots from his face and flung them at James. They grew into full-sized cavum worms and landed at his feet, crawling toward the warmth and emotion that they could smell.

James struck out with the sword, the blue of the blade turning into lightning arcs of electricity that fried each worm it came in contact with, sweeping them into dust as quickly as Gladhands could create them. Adlan and the Baron took on one, protecting James' flank, while the vampire had turned into a bat and was flying just out of reach of another, distracting it.

James rushed forward and swung with his sword, catching the meat of Gladhands' arm and chopping it clean off. Gladhands shrieked as the hand fell to the ground. From out of the gaping wound no blood poured, but rather a thick and chunky mess of worms and maggots, writhing and wriggling. The hand that fell to the ground broke apart into more of the wriggling little worms and crawled back into Gladhands under the leg of his pants. The hand reformed itself within a minute.

If that mouth was capable of an expression, James could swear that it smiled just then at him. "That's no ordinary sword, is it?" Gladhands said as he stood back. "This fight may have to wait for another day. Farewell for now." With that Gladhands broke apart into an entire mound of the maggots and worms that he was made of and slithered into one the arches, disappearing.

*****

"We know where he went, at least," James said as he sheathed his sword. The snow continued to fall, powdering the ground and showing the path that Gladhands had slithered through.

"I'm sorry, child," the Baron said, "but this is where I have to leave you. It was painful to me while we were fighting, that sword stung me even though I fought for your side."

James nodded his head. "I understand. I thank you for getting us this far."

Without another word the Baron transformed into a bat and flew up out of the cavern.

"I still hate the bastard," Chester said, "but it was good of him to fight with us, I'll give him that."

Adlan picked up Jewel and slung her across his back; she had regained a little of her strength, though not much. "Are you up for this?" the giant asked her.

She nodded her head, not bothering with a verbal answer.

"All right," James said, sheathing his sword. "Let's do this." He faced the archway that Gladhands had traveled through, and with a few deep breaths he stepped through.

CHAPTER TWENTY-TWO

It was evening, and snow fell all around him as the others came through the portal. Something was very different about this story; it wasn't a fairy-tale land at all. They were standing on a street corner, a modern street corner, where an inch or so of snow crunched underfoot. An electric streetlight hummed above them, bathing them in a orange glow.

"What sort of enchanted land is this?" Adlan asked, his mouth open as he stared in open-eyed wonder at all the houses. A few people walked along the sidewalks across the street and gave him suspicious glances, but most paid him no mind, their faces buried within hoods against the driving snow.

"It looks like the real world," James said. "Sorry," he corrected himself, "my world. I shouldn't say that mine is the real world. I recognize this, though. I know it from somewhere."

The giant set Jewel down onto her own feet. "I think I'm okay for a little bit," she said, though she shivered with her arms curled tight against herself.

Adlan stepped off the sidewalk and into the street, spreading his arms wide. "What a strange place. The buildings look so square, everyone is dressed so strangely."

James gasped and grabbed the back of Adlan's shirt, pulling

him back up onto the sidewalk just as a car roared past them, honking its horn at the man.

"What in the blazes was that?" Adlan shouted. Some of the people standing around on the sidewalk looked over at him in curiosity. "It looked like a carriage but there were no horses drawing it. What sort of magic would allow that?"

"It's called a car," James said. "And essentially that's what it is. A horseless carriage."

"Oh no," Jewel said, biting at her lip. "I think I know which story this is. I can feel it."

"You do?" James asked, "what happens in it? Is it one of yours?"

A man stumbled from outside of the house across the street from them, almost tripping down the stairs. He hiccuped and swayed as he walked, fumbling to remove keys from his jacket pocket.

"Patrick!" A woman's voice called out. "You're in no condition to drive. Give me the keys, I'll drive us home."

James spun around, his attention grabbed; he knew that voice. Hot tears sprang to his eyes and his breath got caught in his throat. "Mom?" he asked in a whisper.

There she was, just as he remembered her. She was beautiful, her brown hair catching the falling snowflakes. Her eyes, though narrowed in anger, were a haunting shade of green.

Within the span of a heartbeat he recognized what was happening.

James knew the concrete details of how his mother had passed away two years before, in the same way that he knew the earth was round, if he didn't quite understand why. He had a coroner's view of the events. She had been driving his dad home from a family friend's party on slippery roads, and she had lost control of the car.

However, as James was quickly finding out, it was one thing to know it cognitively. It was another altogether to be confronted with it before his eyes. A great sinking pit developed in his stomach as he watched his father drunkenly throw the keys to his mother.

"Patrick," his mother said, her movements jerky and quick, "you promised me you wouldn't drink tonight. It's not my turn to drive home and you know it. Honestly, I can't believe you sometimes."

Patrick slid on a patch of ice and fell onto his backside, letting out a groan. Sitting up, he rubbed at his lower back. "I only had one, Catherine, I can still drive. Besides, it's Jack's birthday, what did you expect me to do? I can't *not* accept a drink he gives me."

Catherine walked over to him and hooked her hands in his armpits, hoisting him up. "Yeah, you could have. And if Jack's as good a friend as you say he is, he wouldn't have minded. But now I had to stay sober because you wouldn't. You're selfish, Patrick, you always have been."

Though she continued to look at him angrily, she helped him to his feet and guided him to the car. Patrick hiccuped and then wiped his lips with the back of his hand. His face looked much younger than the father James knew. The deep lines around the eyes were tiny compared to the ravines they were now. He looked healthier, fuller, his frame not as gaunt and his hands less shaky.

"Is this a memory?" James asked as he watched the scene. "I don't understand. This is all true."

Jewel placed a hand on his shoulder. "No, it's another of his stories."

"But this actually happened," James said.

Jewel tightened her grip on him as they watched Catherine help Patrick into the passenger door and buckle his seat belt for him. She kissed him stiffly on the cheek and he smiled after her, his eyelids drooping closed.

"Think James. Why would your father write something like this?"

James furrowed his brow. That period in his life was hazy. It was strange, he could remember before the accident, could remember his mother when she was alive. She would make him grilled peanut butter sandwiches, cut in triangles. At bedtimes when his father would go down to his study to work she would be there to tuck him into bed; she always tucked him in so snugly he could barely move, and then she would read him a bedtime story, one of his father's. She would even do the voices; they sounded terrible, nothing like they did in his head, but he loved that she did them anyway. His father always had a nickname for her, something precious, but he couldn't quite remember it. It was like hearing the word through a wall; it was too fuzzy, he couldn't make it out. "I don't know," James said.

"I don't like this place," Adlan said. "There's something sinister about it. It's definitely one of the bad stories, though it doesn't seem like it. We should keep moving, keep after Gladhands while he's close."

"Will we recognize his story when we see it?" James asked.

"I think we will," Jewel said, another fit of coughing wracking her body.

"Who is that woman?" Chester asked. "And why do I feel a great affection for her?"

Adlan chuckled and nudged him in the ribs. "You feel a great affection for all women."

Chester frowned at him. "Not all the time. Apparently to you I'm nothing more than a walking phallus with ears. I don't mean that I feel an *attraction* to her, but I feel very affectionately towards her, even though I don't think that we've ever met."

James was about to speak but a large lump caught in his throat. He put his head down, and Jewel spoke for him. "That's James' mother. You may have met her and just not realized."

Chester frowned. "I don't think that's the case. I usually remember a face."

"Faces can change," Jewel said. A car door slammed and they looked over to where James' parents were. Even from outside of the car they could see the animated gestures they were making.

"I didn't realize they were fighting this much," James said.

The car chugged to life. It was an old Volvo that coughed twice before sputtering awake. The gears made a grinding sound as it pulled off onto the street. A red bumper sticker on the back read, 'If this bumper sticker looks blue, you need to slow down.'

"Where are they going?" James asked. "Have you ever been to this story?"

A pained look crossed Jewel's features. The lines around her eyes were set deep, her mouth pursed together so tightly her lips turned white. "I have. I can take you to where they went."

She held his hand tightly as she led him across the street, winding through the backyard of a snowy suburban neighborhood. When they crossed between backyards

250

something shifted; they were still in the same story but the surroundings had changed. James paused, took a step back, and returned to the suburban area.

"It's a different scene," Jewel said and pulled him forward.

The new area James recognized. It was the road leading to his house. They lived out in the country, at the end of a long stretch of road that led up a hill. It was lined on both sides by towering oak trees dusted with snow; they found themselves surrounded by them. The road was covered in the white powder. Home was at the top, and as he looked toward it James was struck by the memory, a summer memory, of riding his bicycle down it at speeds that brought tears to his eyes.

Taking a step, James slipped on a piece of black ice and Jewel reached out a hand to steady him. "Careful, James. It's very slick here."

She led them off the road and into a ditch where they stood in ankle high snow, shivering in the cold.

"What are we waiting here for?" Chester said, his arms crossed over his chest and a shiver running through him. "Out there may have been slippery but at least we weren't buried in this stuff."

They heard the distant rumble of a car coming from down the road. Visibility was poor, the snow fell in thick white sheets, but soon they could see the dim glow of headlights.

As the rusted old Volvo drove by down the road James had another memory bubble up to the surface. He remembered how in the back of that car, old french fries would get lodged in between the seats and stay there for years. His parents were always curious how there were so many french fries back there, but James knew. When he was younger he had a fascination with hiding things, and his young mind thought it was a great idea to hide a snack for later, not really understanding that he wouldn't want to eat week-old fries.

What a strange memory to think of just then, as he watched the car crash that he had heard so much about, the car crash that had killed his mother.

*****

It happened as though in slow motion. The car passed them quickly and hit the same patch of black ice that James had slipped on. It was covered by an inch or so of fresh-fallen snow; there was no way that Catherine could ever have seen it. The car slid one way and then the ice ended, catching the side of the tire and flipping the entire thing. It rolled over and over and flipped into the ditch, slamming into one of the massive oak trees with a screech that set James' teeth on edge.

The car looked like a turtle on its backside, the tire spinning in a wobbly circle, one headlight smashed out. James ran across the road to his parents, slipping on the black ice and landing with all his weight down onto one knee. He cried out in pain and tears sprang to his eyes but he was standing in an instant, limping toward the wreckage.

His father was still buckled in his seat, hanging upside down, a little trail of blood coming from a cut across one eye. His mother had slid through the top buckle, she was half lying outside the car, her legs held in by the seat belt, her head at an impossible angle, the light quickly fading from her green eyes.

"Mom?" James said. "Mom? Mommy?" The pain in his knee faded to an echo and he knelt down beside the broken window of the car. He shook her shoulder; she moved easily with his touch, like a rag doll.

Memories of that time came flooding back to him, things he hadn't thought about since they happened. He remembered how his dress shoes didn't fit, they pinched him throughout the funeral and he told his father three different times that they hurt him. Each time his father would respond, "Okay James, we'll get you different shoes," only to forget about it a moment later. Patrick had a blank, lost look about him, like he was experiencing everything through a fog. James was so frustrated; couldn't anyone see that his shoes hurt?! They pinched his toes and he could barely walk but everyone else was wearing black shoes and black pants and black shirts. There was so much black, why did everyone do that? James didn't understand; his mother hated black clothes; she liked lively colored clothes. Sky blues and forest greens and vibrant yellows; why would everyone wear black when they were saying goodbye to her?

In the weeks after the funeral Patrick would drive James to school and sometimes just wait all day for him, sitting in the car, as though without James telling him where to drive to he didn't know what to do.

The kids at school always asked him why his dad was just sitting in his car outside the school, and he never had an answer for them. The teachers would sometimes go out and talk to Patrick for a minute, though they let him just sit there afterward.

Patrick rarely went to bed the months after it happened; he would fall asleep on the couch with that brown liquid in a glass on the table. James didn't like the sour smell his father accumulated.

A heavy hand grabbed James' shoulder and turned him away from the wreckage. Adlan was there, sitting in front of him with a tear glistening at the corner of his mouth. He cleared his throat and looked James in the eye. "Whatever you're thinking lad, it's in the past. This is a bad story, it's meant to hurt you." He then pulled James into a hug.

"It's not a bad story though," a voice called out.

They turned. Standing in the middle of the road was Gladhands, his mask back in place, his smile large. As he stood the snow formed a little layer on the shoulders of his black suit jacket. Adlan took a step toward the monster. "Now's not the time for you!"

He tugged out his sword from the holster on his back and swung at Gladhands. The man in the suit moved fluidly, stepping to the side just enough for the sword to whistle by harmlessly. In one motion he pulled his white gloves off and pressed a hand to the man's chest. A cavum worm tore voraciously into Adlan.

The giant gasped and turned extremely pale. He sat down gently on the ground, his shoulders slumping and the sword falling from his fingers. His eyes began to droop with sadness.

"Like I was saying, this isn't a bad story," Gladhands said, stepping over Adlan. "I know your father very well, and I haven't changed anything about this story. This is one story that is extremely personal to him, because he didn't write it as a story, he simply wrote it as a memory. This was a way for him to enshrine his pain, to keep it cold for whenever he found himself feeling too happy."

James thrust a finger out at Gladhands. "This is your story, isn't it? This is where you come from!"

Gladhands smiled even larger. "No, child, though I love this story very much. But this isn't my story at all, it's hers," he said, pointing to Jewel.

James took a step away from the both of them. Jewel began to cough, doubling over with the strength of it. Her lips were dotted with red spots when she finally straightened.

"Oh my," Gladhands said, turning to Jewel. "What's this? I wondered how James seemed to be acting so healthy when he should have a nice hole in his heart from the cavum worm, and now I think I know. You took a bit of your own and put it in him, didn't you?" Gladhands said.

Jewel looked like she was about to say something and then coughed again, her breath being robbed from her.

"Oh, how wonderful," Gladhands said. "You know, I thought I was done with you when I thought up the idea to trap you in the witch's story. I should have cut out your tongue rather than just gag you, but in a way this is so much better. I think that it is time for you and me to come to terms with one another."

He drew himself up to his full height, his figure standing like a lightning bolt against the white of the snow. Another fit of coughing wracked Jewel's body as she tried to stand up to match him. He smiled, and James thought he saw something wriggling in the darkness of that mouth.

"Let us match powers against each other, your song against

my worms, and see who truly holds sway over the realms of these stories."

Jewel locked eyes with James; she looked so pale. All the life drained out of her face, but still she held herself tall and puffed out her chest. Her chin was set in a look of grim determination as the snow fell on her shoulders. With a deep breath she opened her mouth and the first notes of her beautiful song fluttered out.

The lyrical music washed over them all like a spring breeze. James could feel his blood warm as he listened to the notes trill high and dip low. They touched minor chords only long enough to make him truly feel the triumph of when she switched back into majors. Something inside of James thawed, and he felt strength as he had never known before, not of arm but of spirit. He knew that if he could hear that song forever then nothing could make him feel sad or small again. It was not pure joy, though. To characterize it as such would be to do it a disservice. There were moments of sorrow in that feeling, but it was the sorrow of a well-lived life, of an acceptance that bad things would happen, but the confidence to know that his spirit was strong enough to see him through anything that would come at him. It was the feeling that it didn't matter that the people he loved might someday be lost; as long as he held on to a piece of them he would have them forever.

Gladhands fell to his knees when he listened to the song, his hands up at his ears, frantically trying to block the noise. His face was set in a look of absolute horror, the mouth gaping, the eyes turned down at the edges, his limbs shaking. He seemed paralyzed by the sound and his form wavered, beginning to turn translucent, as though he were fading from reality itself.

As the song dipped low something changed, one of the notes fell flat and lifeless. The song faltered and Jewel raised a hand to her throat as a little cough worked its way into her voice. The little cough turned larger and larger, and eventually the song stopped because the singer had no breath for anything but a gasping wheeze and a cough. The fragile feeling that had been so gently reinforcing itself all around the group shattered in that instant.

Gladhands smiled and stood, another cavum worm slithering its way out of his hand, snapping at the air around it. "I thought you wouldn't be able to sustain that, not with that hole in your heart. Don't you regret it now? Giving that little piece of yourself to him? You were the only chance that anyone had of beating me, and now you can't even sing. How wonderful." He held up his right hand, the cavum worm wriggling around on it. "I don't think that any normal worm will do for this feast." The cavum worm slid back into his hand and his arm began to twitch. The whole right side of his body wracked back and forth, bulging and growing. Something thick made its way through his arm, tearing through the seams of the suit that Gladhands wore. The opening in his palm grew larger and larger. Soon the head of a monstrous cavum worm birthed its way out of his hand and fell heavily toward the ground. Gladhands gasped with the effort of it, doubled over and breathing heavily.

The gigantic worm slithered its way on the ground over to Jewel, its yellow stare hungry. None of the group seemed to be able to move, their eyes locked onto the worm as it slid forward toward Jewel. Chester pulled his sword from his sheath but the worm fixed him with a stare that seemed to drain all courage out of him. James gripped the hilt of his sword, but the sight of the worm had the effect of sucking every single happy feeling out of his body, leaving him limp and helpless, unable to draw the Arbiter.

The worm slid around Jewel's ankles first, climbing her. She was frozen, pale, unable to move or sing as the thing wound its way higher and higher until it finally reached her breast. It burrowed in just above her heart, its nose parting her flesh and sliding easily into her breast. Her mouth hung limply, her eyes blank and staring up into the sky, the snow falling gently all around her. Though the worm itself was at least four feet long, the entirety of it slid into her chest and the wound closed itself behind it. Jewel fell to her knees. "It's so cold," she said finally, her words soft and weak.

With the worm gone the others found they could move again. James ran to Jewel and held her in his arms as she tipped backward and lay on the ground. He cradled her head in his lap, brushing her black hair away from her eyes.

"You monster!" Chester said, finally finding the strength to pull his sword free. He held it menacingly toward Gladhands. "I challenge you, fiend, to fight a real man instead of picking on women and children!"

Gladhands scoffed. "I can see what women like in you, you're all cock and balls. Unfortunately that leaves little room for brains. Jewel was more powerful than a thousand of you, mouse. Even that great lummox back there is more powerful than you, and look at what both are reduced to. They can't even stand, let alone fight me. What chance do you think you have?"

Chester paled and took a deep breath. "I don't know that I do have a chance. But I can't let you harm an innocent woman and get away with it. Do you accept my challenge or not?"

Gladhands laughed, low at first and then the pitch rose and rose until it was a high shriek. "Yes, brave little mouse, you have earned my attention."

Chester lunged forward, stabbing directly toward Gladhands' heart. His sword struck true, piercing through the monster's chest. The mouse let out a laugh of relief as he buried the tip of the sword into Gladhands. "Looks like I've earned more than your attention," Chester said with a smile on his face. "Do you have any last words before you die?"

Gladhands' smile grew larger. "If I were dying, then I might. Like I said, you have no power over me." He reached out and grasped the hilt of the sword. His arm flexed and he pulled the sword further into his own chest, dragging the mouse closer to him. "Do you really think I have a heart inside this suit? This little bit of metal is nothing to me." His iron grip pulled Chester close and he embraced the mouse, cavum worms coming out of every orifice of his body. They wrapped themselves around the mouse, swarming him, burrowing into him. Gladhands let the mouse go and Chester fell to his knees, his fur trembling as the worms swam around inside him. His one good eye opened wide with horror.

James placed Jewel's head gingerly upon the ground. She had a pulse, though it was weak. He was not doing her, nor anyone else, a favor by staying there cradling her. Drawing his sword from his sheath, he stood. The blade of the Arbiter shone brightly, casting a blue hue upon everything.

"Now *this* should be interesting," Gladhands said. "A child, all alone, against the prince of sadness. Who do you think you are to face me if all your friends, those who were written for struggle, stood no chance at all?"

The tip of the sword shook as he held it out in front of him, but he stood his ground. "I've heard the whispers of your little pets, heard your voice through them. And now you've put them in my friends. I can only imagine the damage you've done to my dad by now. I have to get back to him, and the only way to do that is to defeat you."

The monster smiled, his eyes softening. "My child, do you just want to go back?" Gladhands asked. "Is that why you're fighting so hard? If it is, if all this frightens you too much, I'll give you an easy out. The gateway to the next story is right in the back of that car," he said, pointing to the upturned Volvo. "That leads to my story, and I can keep everything from touching you there, I have that power. The page is on my desk. You can take it, and you can travel back home. After all, you're just a child, you shouldn't have to deal with any of this. Go back to your innocence, go back to your childhood. Go back and play with your friends, leave troubles like this to older heads than yours."

James' resolve began to waver. He could go home now if he wanted to, he didn't have to travel through these stories any more. It all seemed like such an easy choice, he could just walk out of here. What chance did he really have against this king of nightmares anyway? A moan came from Jewel's lips, like a scream that had been muffled by a pillow.

A hungry look flashed across Gladhands' face. A chill ran down the length of James' spine.

"No," James said.

Gladhands tipped his ear towards the child. "What was that?"

"I said no," James repeated.

Gladhands frowned at him. "What do you mean, no?"

James stepped toward Gladhands and raised the tip of the sword. His knees were shaking and his stomach felt like it was tumbling around inside of him, but he gripped the sword hard and forced himself to step closer. "I will be returning to my world, but not before I defeat you. I don't believe a word you say. You're trying to trick me, to get me to think I can't win. Well I can, and I will."

Gladhands side-stepped until he was right in front of the car door. He opened it with one hand and slid backward into it. "Well in that case I'll see you in my story." As soon as Gladhands stepped foot into the car he disappeared.

James checked on all his friends. They were ashen and pale, their breathing coming slowly and their pulses weak, but they were alive. He huddled them together, hoping that they would grant each other some sort of warmth, and prepared himself to step through the car door into Gladhands' story.

CHAPTER TWENTY-THREE

There are two very different types of bravery that we all have, to varying degree. The first is well known, it is the bravery we feel when we are together. While surrounded by a group of our peers it is easy to feel brave; we feed off each other's emotions and find ourselves bolstered by it. That type of bravery certainly has its merits, don't get me wrong, but it is an easier bravery than the one that James had to summon while standing in front of the open car door.

James had to summon the other type of bravery, a bravery one gets from inside. You see, many people who are brave in crowds are cowards by themselves. It takes a special type of person to stand alone before the darkness and willingly step forward. They have to have that courage within themselves; they draw upon their own power rather than soaking it up from a group.

*****

With a few deep breaths, James stepped into the back of the upturned car. He landed on soft, shifting brown soil, and when he registered what was all around him he felt his stomach sour in fear. Nightmare creatures surrounded him, glaring at him, flashing teeth and claws at him. There were minotaurs with great bloody axes and translucent girls with dead skin; demons with too many eyes and lizards with blood dripping from their mouths. Every imaginable nightmare a child has ever had surrounded him, towering over him.

The fear he should have experienced was dulled slightly by the shield over his heart, but most of it went through him, leaving him feeling cold and small. His heart raced as the nightmare creatures began to crowd around him, stepping closer and closer.

A sudden hush filled the room as a song began. The back of James' neck tingled as he listened to the low, sad notes. As it climbed in pitch he recognized it; it was Jewel's song, though he didn't see her anywhere around.

The effect it had on the nightmare creatures was instantaneous; they backed swiftly away, cowering from the noise. James' courage was boosted and he lifted his glowing sword up. Every time he moved, the song moved with him. Where was Jewel singing from?

He took a step toward them and they disappeared, having been nothing but the stuff of shadows, leaving him able to see all around.

He was in a large hall, the ground sloping all the way around a stage erected in the middle. It was an empty theater; no one occupied the seats though a light shone upon the stage. With everyone gone the song quieted down to a hum, and James realized with a gasp where it was coming from.

Just behind his breastplate his heart continued to murmur Jewel's song. With his courage bolstered, he set off down the steps towards the stage. As he neared the center he could see more details about the wooden platform. There were blood-red curtains hanging around the stage, parted and tied up with a golden sash. Toward the back of the stage a vanity stood with several masks mounted to one side, each of which depicted a different emotion. In the center of the stage, where the spotlight shone the brightest, Gladhands stood. He was smiling.

"I had rather hoped that they would put up more of a fight than that," Gladhands said as James climbed the stage. He winced as James got closer. "Ah, the song. Interesting."

"How much of you is just an illusion?" James asked, the sword down by his side. "Do you have any substance at all?"

Gladhands walked to the vanity and unbuckled his face, pulling it off and replacing it with one of open-eyed earnestness. When it was buckled securely he opened a drawer and pulled out a book. "This is it, you know, the thing that you came for. It's the gateway back to your world. Here, take it," Gladhands said, holding the open book out toward James.

Through the page he could see the ceiling to his father's study, the cracked spackling that Patrick always said he was going to fix.

"Why would you give it to me now? Is it because you know you are beaten?" James asked.

The earnest-faced mask that Gladhands now wore was deeply disconcerting. It didn't bother hiding the hunger nor the glee that Gladhands displayed. With a little titter of a laugh, the monster clapped his hands together. "Beaten? Me? My dear child, I believe I have already won. You are truly becoming just like me, so cold and emotionless inside."

James hadn't expected this; he stopped mid-stride. "What are you talking about? I'm nothing like you."

"Oh but you are," Gladhands said, motioning him toward the mirror mounted in the vanity. "Look at what you have done."

James approached the large oval mirror. The image of himself approaching shimmered and then changed, showing the car crash from the previous story. Adlan, Chester, and Jewel all lay on the ground together, perfectly still, just where he had left them, though none of their chests were rising or falling. "Are they...dead?" James asked.

"Yes," Gladhands said. "They died because you left them there alone. You couldn't even take five minutes to get them back to the previous story, where they would have been warmer. They all froze to death because of you; isn't that just wonderful?"

"That's a lie!" James shouted. "You did that, and now you're blaming me!"

"And look at you now," Gladhands continued, "you're more concerned for whose fault it is rather than the fact that your friends are dead." Snake-like, he crept behind James and pointed into the mirror. The hot smell of decay was on his breath as he talked. "Do you want to truly know your level of self-involvement?"

"What do you mean?" James asked. "I'm not self-involved at all, this whole thing is to help my dad."

Gladhands gripped him tightly on the shoulder and pointed again to the mirror. "Yes, but you didn't even notice who Jewel was, did you? Don't you remember me telling you that it was her story? Wouldn't that seem weird for a princess to be in a story about a car wreck? Well, you may have consciously forgotten about it, but I've been in your heart; I've seen things you don't even remember." The glass shimmered again and an image of a cradle appeared. It was being rocked steadily by a woman in a purple shawl. It was his mother, though she looked younger than he had ever seen her. She had no lines around her eyes, though they had the same soft affection in them. She was singing to him, a soft song that sounded painfully familiar. James had heard it before, had heard it from Jewel and from the piece of her that filled the hole in his heart.

James gasped and took a step away from the mirror. Jewel couldn't be his mother; she looked nothing like her. The face was completely different. Of course, James thought, the personality certainly matched with what his mother had been. Caring and nurturing, willing to sacrifice her own health and happiness for his. And the song, hadn't he known it along? Hadn't he recognized it? Hadn't some part of him cried out with happiness every time he heard it?

"Oh, he didn't write her to look exactly like your mother. He wrote her as he saw her, as a princess," Gladhands said. "And you left her to die. You were more than willing to take a piece of her heart, crippling her, leaving her vulnerable to me, all because you couldn't handle your own problems."

James fell to his knees and he knew it to be true. Why else would she have taken a piece of herself and put it in him? That was a motherly act, a noble sacrifice that he didn't deserve. What had he done?

Gladhands knelt beside him and placed a hand on his shoulder. "And that's why I'm giving the book to you. You're done here, you've become like me by your own actions. Here, go home." Once again he set the book before James.

The mirror on the vanity still showed his mother singing to him in his cradle. She rocked him gently back and forth, her voice soothing him to sleep, and something unexpected happened. As she sang his heart followed suit, matching song to song, rising in volume.

Just as before, when his heart's song had caused all the nightmare creatures to disappear, the song filled him with courage. A warmth spread throughout his body and he felt powerful enough to stand and lift his blade. "It's lies, you're nothing but lies. That's your power, you take the truth and you magnify the bad parts and diminish the good." He stepped toward Gladhands, his sword glowing with its own energy.

"Ah," Gladhands said as he held up a finger, backing away slowly, "but isn't that just a matter of perspective? You really did leave all your friends to freeze out there in the cold. You just didn't care about that as much as I did. Go home, James, there's nothing more that you can do here. You can't kill me, I'm a part of too many stories, I can't die."

James paused for a moment, his sword at his waist. "You can't die?"

Gladhands shook his head slowly. "No. Do what you will, but I will never go away."

The glow of the Arbiter intensified until it was painful to look at, and James watched as Gladhands held a hand up and backed away. "This can hurt you, though, can't it?" James said with a smile. He lunged forward, feinting one way and then sweeping at Gladhands' legs. The blade bit into the suit pants and knocked the monster off his feet. "You weren't hurt by Chester's sword, but you are by this."

Gladhands fell heavily onto his back and James was on top of him in an instant, raising his sword high and bringing it plunging down into the middle of Gladhands. The sword itself must have lent its own power to James, because it did more than simply pierce through Gladhands' body; it went through both the body and the wood of the stage, all the way into the rock underneath. It lodged itself firmly in the ground, the light emanating from it almost blinding in its intensity.

Gladhands' entire body tensed and writhed, it curled back on itself like the legs of a dying spider. His face was one of absolute horror, the blue light of the sword illuminating every single little shadow on him. He shrieked and tugged at the blade, but it wouldn't move a millimeter and burned his hands every time he tried. He was stuck, mounted to the ground like an insect. "Take it out! Take it out!" he shrieked.

"You'll stay here, stuck in your own story," James said, "never again able to infect the others."

James picked up the book and took one last look at Gladhands. The monster was reaching toward him with little gasps and moans, unable to move the blade from his chest.

With one last look toward the stage James turned his back and walked away.

*****

His friends were sitting up in the snow when he arrived. Their eyes were alert and they smiled when they saw him. "How are you guys feeling?" James asked.

Jewel stood and rubbed at her chest. "Much better. That hole inside me disappeared a few minutes ago; can I assume you had something to do with that?"

James nodded. "He's not dead, but I pinned him there so he can't leave his story."

"I don't hear his little nagging thoughts anymore," Chester said as he picked up his sword and sheathed it. "I didn't think I'd ever have my sanity back."

"That was hell," Adlan said. "I can't imagine hearing those thoughts all the time, just picking apart everything about you. It just took the fight right out of me." He hung his head and avoided their eye contact. "I'm sorry I dropped so quickly. I should have been able to help more than that."

James placed a hand on his shoulder. "It's not your fault; there was something inside of you eating away at everything you are, but it's gone now. It's not your fault at all."

Adlan smiled and a blush rose to his cheeks. "Aw, come here!" he shouted and he swooped up James in a great big bear hug.

When he was finally set down James patted at the book. "We should get going, there's someone I'm anxious to see."

The party agreed and they headed off toward the gate, beginning the long trek home. James fell to the back and tugged on Jewel's arm to do the same. When they had lagged far enough behind the others, James stopped them both and looked hard into Jewel's face.

"What is it?" Jewel asked.

In that moment he could see it, he could see his mother in Jewel. It was in the way she brushed her hair behind her ear, the melodious tone of her voice, the soft touch of her hands. This princess before him was how his father saw her, how he had known her his entire life. "Why didn't you tell me who you were?" James asked.

Jewel's smile faded. "I had the feeling that someday I might not be able to continue, and that if I were to tell you who I really was, you wouldn't let me fall behind. And I'm not *really* your mother, you know. I just have a whole lot of her in me. Nothing could truly be her except herself."

James nodded; he thought he understood. As close as it was,

it wasn't reality; or maybe, this was a different reality from the one outside of the stories. Even the woman in the car wasn't really his mom, just as the man wasn't really his dad. He had the sudden and fierce desire to get back home, to see his father and just give him a hug and let him know that he didn't have to hate himself for what happened, that it was over and done with and not his fault. It was ice, simple dumb-luck black ice that had caused it; it didn't matter that his dad had drunk a few too many and had Catherine drive. None of it was his fault.

"Guys," he said, stopping Chester and Adlan in their tracks, "I have to go home."

The three turned and looked upon him with kindness in their eyes. "I figured this was coming," Adlan said, "as soon as I saw you had that book in your hands. Will you come and visit us occasionally?"

James' eyes watered and for a moment he couldn't see. He blinked away the tears and cleared his throat. "Of course I will. I'll come see all of you."

"You should come to my story," Chester said. "I'll teach you all you need to know about women."

"I will," James laughed. He gave Chester and Adlan a hug before they stepped back and allowed him a moment with Jewel.

"You won't forget about me here, will you?" Jewel said, kneeling down to look him in the eye.

James smiled. "I don't think that I even could. I'll take you guys with me forever, and I promise to visit as often as I can."

Jewel gave him a hug; her arms felt too familiar, and the tears that he had blinked away earlier came back with reinforcements. When she let him go he wiped them away with the back of his hand.

He placed the book on the ground and opened it to the page he had entered on. The ceiling on his father's study was dark, all the lights off. How long had he been away? Days? Months? Did time in the story correlate to time outside? Hopefully his dad wasn't too worried about him, it would be a hard thing to explain all that had happened.

James smiled and waved at his traveling companions before stepping through the page.

*****

Stumbling out onto his father's desk, he blinked in the darkness. Outside the window the trees were beginning to seep a red orange light through their branches.

"James?" a voice called out from down the hall. "Is that you?"

James walked out of the office and tiptoed down the hall.

The living room light was on; as James entered the room he saw his father awake on the couch, pen and paper in hand, a glass of water on the table in front of him.

"Dad?" James asked. "What are you doing awake?"

His father smiled at him. The lines of sorrow and worry that had lined the corners of his eyes were all but gone. "What am I doing awake? I should ask you the same thing. I thought you went to bed hours ago. How long have you been up?"

James went and sat by his father on the couch, leaning up against him. "I don't know, have I been gone long?"

Patrick held him at arm's length, a slight smile at the corner of his mouth. "Gone? You went to bed at ten last night. How'd you get into my office?"

"The door was unlocked," James said. "I'm sorry, I know you don't like it when I go in there."

Patrick shrugged and took a sip of water. "Oh, I don't mind, not really. Sorry if I got cranky with you the other day when I found you in there, I haven't been feeling myself lately."

"Are you feeling okay now?" James asked.

His father was about to answer, and then a puzzled look came over his face. His brow furrowed and he looked lost in deep concentration. "You know," he said when he finally answered, "I am. I felt off for a long time, but I woke up a little while ago and I just sort of felt right again. Doesn't that sound

276

weird?"

James shook his head. "It's not weird at all. What are you writing about?"

The page was blank in his father's lap. "Your guess is as good as mine, but I really feel like working on something today. What's a story I should write?"

James hugged his father close. "Write a story about mom. A good story."

Patrick looked taken aback. His brow furrowed again and then he nodded. "I used to write about her a lot, you know. I always made her a princess."

"I know," James said. "I like those stories, but can you write one about her in real life? About what she was like?"

Patrick nodded and then smiled. "Sure Bud, I suppose I can."

*****

I didn't start this with a 'Once upon a time,' and I'm not going to end it with a 'Happily ever after.' Gladhands isn't the type of monster that you can kill, but he is the type of monster that you can deal with. There's a Gladhands inside everyone, waiting patiently, whispering. If you look inside yourself and find that he has escaped, don't worry. You have everything you need to put him back where he belongs.

THE END

Author Biography

Andrew J. Krause was born in Madison, Wisconsin, and grew up a child of the woods, a dreamer of dragons and a friend of the fantastic. In early 2013 he woke up from a deep sleep, a sleep low enough for him to slumber amongst the subconscious. He had been dreaming of a forest like the one of his childhood, but one where every tree was twisted and tangled into things darker than shadows. In the middle of a moonlit glade the creature who would eventually become Gladhands waited. With the smile of a jackal it reached toward him and held his heart in its icy fingers. When he woke it was with the fevered desire to draw the thing that had attacked him. The following picture formed the basis for this novel.